a day at the beach

a day at the the beach

Richard Adelman

new texture

For Jake and Andy

CONTENTS

Blessings on thee, little man,
Barefoot boy, with cheek of tan!

Prologue

IT'S THE day of my annual visit to Atlantic City.

I'm from Philly, but from the time I was two months old until I was thirty-eight, I spent my summers in the Inlet section of Atlantic City. My family had a summer home there. We vacated Philadelphia the day after school ended and didn't return until the day before school began. We never missed a summer.

When I was a kid, my summers were idyllic. To really appreciate the seashore, a kid needs to spend the whole summer. A couple of weeks won't do. The first two weeks at the shore are just preparation. First, you have to get the terrible sunburn that you need for the tan that will protect you from future sunburns. Then, you need to run around on the sand and rock piles enough to get the callouses on your feet you need to go barefoot all day. Finally, you have to brine yourself in the ocean for long hours every day—no matter what the ocean temperature—until your lips are the color of plums, so you are hardened against any temperature or roughness the ocean might present. After a couple of weeks, you're ready to enjoy the rest of the summer. I was chestnut brown, shod with callouses, and seasoned with salt water by July 4*th*, and after that came halcyon days, one after another.

It all ended when I started working during the summer. I got to know the business end of Atlantic City. It wasn't pretty. For more than twenty years I worked long hours in seashore restaurants. I was a busboy, a waiter, a bartender, and finally a restaurant manager. When I was in school, I worked to provide myself with spending money for the winter. Then when I became a teacher, I worked to supplement my salary. Because I had my summers free when I was a student and then a teacher, I was the perfect hire for a seashore restaurant. I showed up when the boss needed help and left *when he needed to lay everyone off.*

After thirty-eight summers, I knew Atlantic City pretty well. Until I retired from my summer jobs and stopped going down the shore, I could have even called myself a local. In the '80s, I recall going to a theater in Philadelphia with some friends to see Louis Malle's film, Atlantic City—a film with an in-depth understanding of the place— and I bothered everyone around us with a running commentary on almost every scene. The audience had to shush me a few times. I said, "Look, there's the gladiola garden across from Haddon Hall where I threw up when I was ten" and "I remember when they built that parking elevator" and "That's the White Horse Pike...or maybe it's the Black Horse Pike...." Noticing that Burt Lancaster and Susan Sarandon lived in the Vermont Apartments, I drew the loudest censure from the audience when I pointed at the screen and blurted, "That's my street!" We lived on Vermont Avenue, which is one of the least expensive properties on the Monopoly board.

Nowadays, I'm a stranger in Atlantic City. But once every summer, I take a day trip, a sentimental journey. I walk on the boardwalk to see how things have changed. Then I sit on the beach for a few hours. I may even dive into the ocean and body-surf a wave or two, if the water's warm enough and looks clean. Walking on the boardwalk, I recognize the ghosts of old buildings hiding inside new buildings. Inside Bally's Park Place Casino lurks the former Marlboro-Blenheim Hotel, where my friends and I, with sandy feet, snuck into the palatial game room and shot pool on the fancy claw-footed tables. Passing where the Steeplechase Pier used to be, I get a whiff of the hot grease that lubricated the wheels of the bumper cars mingled with the smell of caramel corn.

Today, after walking the boards, I was on my way down the wooden steps that lead to the beach, and I saw something that triggered a surge of nostalgia. Close to the wooden steps, in the hot sand at the top of Montgomery Avenue beach, three kids, wet from the ocean, were lying on their bellies, facing one another in a tight circle, getting sandy and having an animated conversation. And there I was, when I was twelve, with my Inlet friends, in an identical circle....

1.
Atlantic City, 1963

BIG NED looked at Whitey and said, "You go."

"No way," said Whitey. "Let Richie go."

"Not me," I said. "I don't want to."

We had just come out of the ocean where the waves were choppy and cold. It was the middle of July, and though the sand had reached the full temperature of summer, the ocean lagged behind. To warm up, we ran to the part of the beach furthest from the water. There, we pressed ourselves into the hot sand.

"You have to go, Richie," said Frankie. "We need the net I keep in CJ's back yard."

"What net?" asked Big Ned.

Frankie answered as though we should all know. "The fishing net."

I dug into the hot sand. "Why me? I'm comfortable."

"Look," said Frank, "I want CJ to come with us. But he never comes out unless we stop up for him. Now, me and Big Ned and Whitey," he pointed to each, "have been taking turns stopping up for CJ all year long. But you just came down for the summer. So you missed all your turns. It's your turn."

Frankie's logic was indisputable. I laid my chin in the sand, sighed, and rose from my warm bed. "OK, I'll go, but I won't like it. CJ's a little strange, and so are his sisters. All of them. How many sisters does he have, anyway?" I brushed the sand from my chest and noticed how the Coast Guard tower on the boardwalk above the Oriental Avenue jetty shimmered like a mirage in the afternoon heat.

"Don't forget the net," said Frankie. "We're going to need it when we get to Brigantine." Frankie looked up at me and squinted, sand on his wet eyelashes. "You ever fish with a net?"

I shook my head.

"Sixteen," said Whitey. Ned chuckled.

"Sixteen what?" I asked.

"Sixteen sisters," said Whitey, and we all laughed.

"Wait 'til you fish with a net. It's boss." Frankie looked at Whitey and Big Ned for support.

Whitey nodded absently, pulling a pillow of warm sand up to his chest, but Big Ned said, "I can't go."

Frankie winced. "Can't go?"

"Got a game tonight. Gotta get ready."

Big Ned was the pitcher for a Little League team at Venice Park, on the mainland. He was considered the best pitcher in the league, or any Little League in America, most likely. And no wonder. At eleven years old, he looked seventeen. He was nearly six feet tall, and he had real muscles.

"All right," Frankie allowed, "Koufax can't go. But you guys are in, right? We'll pedal over. Easy ride."

Whitey said, "I'm in. Dad's home with Chip today." Whitey was generally game for an adventure if he didn't have to look after his little brother.

I said, "Sure," even though my mother strictly prohibited my taking side trips from the area around Vermont Avenue without her permission, and she would never allow me to go as far as Brigantine on my bike. She didn't allow a lot of things, which was why I never asked permission.

"You know where CJ lives?" Frank asked.

"I know it to see it, I think. On Rhode Island."

"104 South. Next to Wasserman's Butcher Shop. In the basement."

"You can't miss it," said Big Ned. "The door is always wide open."

"I hope his sisters aren't there," I turned and trudged toward the steps leading to the boardwalk. Behind me, I heard Frankie say, "C'mon guys."

From the boardwalk, I could see my summer friends navigating single file around people's blankets back to the cold water. Frankie marched in advance. Big Ned, a foot taller than the others, strode behind him. Whitey, somehow still untanned, took up the rear, stepping gingerly on the hot sand and holding his arms aloft like a seagull.

We had left our bikes leaning on the boardwalk rail. I untangled mine from the others. It was a red Schwinn, stripped of everything but brakes and aged to a dull brown from spending winters in the storage room of our summer home. It had been my older brother's, and his older brother's. The first thing I did each summer when we arrived in Atlantic City was oil the bearings, grease the chain, air up the tires, and take a few laps on the boardwalk up to Oriental Avenue to bring the big old Schwinn back to life.

Climbing aboard, the pedals were hot, so I pushed with the tips of my toes, and I thumped down the boardwalk in the direction of Rhode Island Avenue.

I lived on Vermont Avenue, which was the first street I passed on my way to CJ's. Except for CJ, all my friends lived on Vermont. Big Ned lived with his mother and father in a basement apartment near the beach. Whitey lived a little further down the block, in a basement too, with his little brother and their father. And Frankie lived further down the street, two doors from me, in a second floor apartment with his aunt, whom he called Rita—not Aunt Rita, just Rita—and his sister Pat, whom I never saw. They lived in Atlantic City all year round which, to me, was incredible. In my life, I'd come to Atlantic City only once during the off-season. My parents needed to check out something at the house. It was almost winter. The windblown beach was empty, and the only sound on the boardwalk was the repetitive clang of a halyard against a distant flagpole. There was nothing doing, and I couldn't imagine how someone could survive the lonely winter.

Pedaling into the welcome shade of the Vermont Apartments at the top of Vermont Avenue, I looked down onto the beach to see if my mother and brother were looking my way. They always sat in the same spot on Vermont Beach, and there they were. My mom was ankle-deep in the ocean, involved in a lively conversation with another lady. She was telling a story, gesturing with her arms, and the other woman was laughing. Unfortunately, I caught the attention of my brother Harry who was sitting at the foot of Mom's beach lounger eating a peach. I waved innocently as I glided by, and Harry waved back. Then, he rose from his seat, most likely to report to Mom that he'd spotted me. I sped off.

Passing the miniature golf course at Victoria Avenue, I slowed my bike and looked through the fence to see who was playing golf. Izzy Goldfarb's three grandchildren, all dressed in the same white polo shirts and white shorts, were teeing off at the hole with the windmill. These kids, two boys and a girl, stayed on Vermont Avenue for a few weeks each summer in Goldfarb's Guest House, but they never said a word to us. They kept to themselves and swam at a classier beach down the island. The girl was pretty. She looked like Natalie Wood, only with a lot of frizzy hair.

Pressing the pedals again, I rounded the corner past the Boardwalk Motel and coasted down the ramp onto Rhode Island Avenue. I skidded to a noisy stop on the corner of Rhode Island and Oriental, where a fan in the transom window of Wasserman's Kosher Butcher Shop blew a strong meaty smell onto the street. Inside, Mr. Wasserman, wrapped in his bloody white smock, leaned on his butcher's block and looked at me suspiciously as I set my bike against a pole outside his window. Wasserman was a holocaust survivor who knew my mother because she bought kosher chickens at his shop.

CJ's place was next to the butcher. He lived in a run-down building covered in reddish asphalt tiles that were supposed to look like bricks. As predicted, the door to CJ's apartment was wide open, so I looked inside. The dim blue light of a TV screen illuminated a small living room. Mingled with the familiar underground smell of mildew and salty dampness that pervaded every basement in Atlantic City, CJ's apartment exhaled an odor of sweaty sheets, cigarette smoke, and Chef Boyardee. A tiny blonde girl in a wet bathing suit sat on the floor in the light of the television and ate Sugar Smacks from the box. I knocked on the doorjamb to get her attention.

"Is CJ here?" I asked.

The little girl turned. She was cross-eyed. "C'mon in," she piped. I stepped just inside the doorway. She set down her box of Smacks and disappeared behind a quilt that hung from a clothesline and separated the very public living room from the private inner rooms.

The Three Stooges, dressed like cowboys, ran around on the TV. All three Stooges at once attempted to jump onto one horse from a second story balcony, and they missed. Moe was angry and knocked Curly's and Larry's heads together. As always, I laughed. On the wall above the TV hung a ceramic Jesus on a wooden crucifix. Jesus was coated with that greenish glow-in-the-dark stuff you see on the hands of watches, and he had a terrible red wound below his chest. Nearby hung a picture of a man in a soldier's uniform.

CJ emerged from behind the blanket. He held it open and took a bow. As usual, he was dressed in tight blue jeans and a short-sleeved shirt with the sleeves rolled up. His duck's ass hairstyle was perfect, and his pointy shoes were black. He wore this outfit everywhere, including to the beach and riding his bike. I never saw him in shorts or swim trunks, and he never swam. He rolled his eyes if we invited him to go swimming. As he held the room divider open, his little sister ran underneath his arm and resumed her place in front of the TV.

"Richard," beamed CJ, cocking his head. "What brings you here?"

My attention, though, was not on CJ and his entrance. Instead, I was looking behind CJ, behind the blanket he held up. There, through an open door, in a lighted bedroom, I could see his older sister, another blonde, and she was naked from the waist up. Her back faced me, and on one side of her lower back she had a bruise the color of a plum and just as big. She was smoking and ironing a waitress uniform. Her hair swayed lightly on her shoulders as she moved her iron back and forth. She was talking with someone, her mom I suppose, who was invisible to me, though I could see the smoke from another cigarette curling upward. They were arguing over who was more exhausted.

"Richard?" CJ repeated. He turned to see what held my attention, and then he rolled his eyes and let the blanket fall. I blushed. Two more of CJ's sisters—twins, I think, about eight or nine—shot from behind the curtain, laughing, as though they were playing tag. They sat together in an arm chair and looked me over. Then they whispered back and forth and disappeared again behind the curtain. "Three Blind Mice," the Stooges' theme song, played on the TV.

I remembered my reason for being there. "Are you going to Brigantine with us, CJ?"

CJ took a cigarette from behind his ear and lit up. He leaned back against the wall. "Brigantine? I can't imagine whose idea that was?"

Missing his sarcasm, I said, "Frankie's. I'm going, and so's Whitey. Big Ned can't go."

Yet another of CJ's sisters came through the curtain, this one a little plump and squirrely-faced, around my age. She sat in the armchair and scrutinized me, making me uncomfortable. She wore a man's white shirt with the top two buttons open, and there were wet patches on the shirt from her bathing suit underneath.

"Really? What's Ned's problem?" CJ asked.

"He's got a game."

"Are you a Jew?" asked CJ's sister in the chair.

"Yeah."

From the floor, without taking her eyes off the TV, CJ's tiny sister mumbled, "Jews killed Jesus."

CJ felt my discomfort. "Who invited you, Marie?"

Marie did not respond. She kept her eyes on me.

"So Big Neddie will hit a few homers for his mummy, huh? And where is everyone now? Looks like the beach," said CJ.

"Yup."

"Ugh," said CJ, breathing out smoke and pressing the curly front of his DA.

"I like Jews," said CJ's sister in the chair. "Do you have a place in Florida?"

"No. Just Philly and Atlantic City," I said.

"I know you like Danny Wasserman," said CJ to his sister.

Marie stood. "Don't you?" she said, and she went back through the curtain, stopping to pull CJ's ear.

"Ow!" CJ almost dropped his cigarette. The tiny sister turned to watch this, finding it more amusing than the TV. She beamed.

"How about the net?" I asked.

"What net?"

"Frankie said you have a fishing net. We're going to use it when we get to Brigantine."

"You mean that filthy pile of rope Frank hid in the back yard?"

"I guess."

"It stinks," CJ wrinkled his nose. Then he shrugged. "I'll get it, but you have to carry it."

"OK."

CJ swung behind the room divider slowly enough for me to see that his sister had finished her ironing and was no longer there. "I'll meet you out front," CJ said from behind the blanket. His sister Marie reappeared after CJ disappeared.

"What's your name?"

"Richie," I said. "You know Danny Wasserman?"

"He's my next door neighbor, dummy."

"Oh, yeah. How many sisters does CJ have?"

"Including himself?" Marie quipped, and I could hear laughter from behind the curtain.

CJ tapped me on my shoulder from behind. He was on the pavement, leading his bike by the handlebars. The net rested on the seat. His bike must have been handed down to him by one of his sisters. It was a pink girls' bike with white grips and a white seat. I wouldn't be caught dead on it. But CJ rode it, and no one said a word about it. At least it was old and battered. He grimaced and said, "Take this awful thing off my bike." He threw the net onto my bike's frame. I noticed he had stuck a new cigarette behind his ear. Marie had come outside and sat on the steps that led to the second story of their building."Where ya goin'?" she asked, squinting.

"None of your fucking business," said CJ good-naturedly.

I took the fishy net and draped it over my shoulder. As we straddled our bikes, I asked, "Could we take the avenue instead of the boardwalk? My mom's on the beach and if she sees me with this net she's liable to think it's part of some dangerous stunt that's sure to end with me either dead or in jail."

"The avenue it is," CJ said, "just don't go too fast…my hair."

"What about it?"

"Ma just gave him a cut. Nice, huh?" Marie smiled at me.

I made as if to touch CJ's precious curl and he pushed my hand away. "Just go on," he said.

Riding back toward New Hampshire Ave. beach, I thought about CJ's sister's bare back and her big bruise. I reexamined the memory carefully to see if I'd caught a glimpse of her breasts—like from the side. Then I thought about Marie. I liked Marie. She had a sense of humor. And a nice smile. And she may have had breasts. They appeared as wet marks made by her bathing suit under the man's shirt.

"How old's Marie?" I asked CJ. We were pedaling abreast in the center of Oriental Avenue, which never had traffic in the middle of a hot afternoon.

He threw me a look. "Twelve. Why?"

"Just wondering."

Thinking about breasts led me to thinking about how we had sneaked up to one of the Western-style swinging doors on the side of the Globe Burlesque Theater a few nights before and peeked through to watch Busty Russell's striptease. I'd been reimagining Busty's dance for the past few nights as I drifted off to sleep. Busty started her routine by sashaying back and forth across the stage wearing a red evening gown. She assumed a look of sophistication, sporting a long cigarette holder and high platinum hair. The band played a waltz, and Busty made a few modest passes across the stage, winking demurely at the crowd. But then, suddenly, the drummer struck a loud boom on the kettledrum, and Busty's fancy gown, as though from a powerful gust of wind, flew up into the curtains above, leaving her naked except for pasties and a g-string. The band swung into something brassy as Busty threw her cigarette holder backstage and began her hoochie-coochie dance. She wiggled up and down, holding her enormous breasts in her hands, cooing at the audience. She stood spread-eagle and laughed. She made the tassels that hung from the tips of her pasties do figure-8s. Every move drew whistles and shouts—from the men in the audience anyway—especially when she arose from a squat and grunted like she was lifting a cinder block. At the door, peeking in, at first, we watched Busty's change from sophisticated lady to naked lady in silent awe, and then, as she strutted and bounced and did tricks with her fabulous bosom, we laughed with approval. "Her tits! Her tits!" said Frankie. "I'd like to get my face in there and—" he flapped his lips to make a blubbering noise. We laughed so loud the usher came and chased us away.

I adjusted my swim trunks to accommodate the changes that thinking about all this inspired.

I wondered then: If I had a choice whether to spend a night with Busty Russell or CJ's sister Marie, which one would I choose? Busty, I thought, was a little scary, with her overripe adult body and her intimidating expressions. Marie was less threatening. Her sense of humor was a little threatening, but nothing like Busty's flirtatious winking and total immodesty. Mainly, Marie won the competition because of one very important thing. Marie was real, and Busty was like someone on TV. Busty's silver pasties and tiny g-string were sexy, but in an artificial way. Marie, slightly plump, in her man's shirt that came down to her knees, with wet marks made by her bathing suit, was cute—in a real way. What's more, Marie had spoken to me. Busty, who most likely had six boyfriends that followed her from town to town, would only chuckle if I said hello.

"Hey, CJ," I asked, "how many sisters do you have?"

"Don't know. Never counted." CJ slouched in his bicycle seat, steering with one hand and smoking with the other.

To get to Brigantine we rode toward the mainland on Maryland Avenue. Maryland became Absecon Road, a causeway through the wide wetlands outside AC. A big sign at Huron Road told us to turn right to get to Brigantine. At last we came to a bridge made of wood, like a wide boardwalk supported by concrete pilings. This was the Brigantine Bridge, a skimpy structure, considering it was the access route for all traffic to and from Brigantine. When we crossed the wooden bridge we entered the town, but not the busy part. That was further along.

We had pedaled about eight miles.

Riding along Heron Road beyond the Brigantine Bridge you felt like you were riding in a desert. It was quiet, the wetlands became beach, and high sand dunes bordered both sides of the road. Over the dunes on one side of the road, was a natural beach, which bordered the bay. Though the water here was calmer and warmer than the water in the ocean, no one swam here. Inviting as it was, only sandpipers, seagulls, and herons used it. The high dunes were discouraging to tourists.

The resort part of Brigantine was further up the road, where the beach was flat and faced the ocean. It was a normal seashore resort, full of summer homes and guesthouses. We visited the beaches in this section from time to time. The waves here were tamer than the waves in Atlantic City, and the water seemed cleaner. Swimming at Brigantine was a treat. At one Brigantine beach, there was a diving platform and a high water slide. Frankie told us the beaches in Brigantine were private, that non-residents were not allowed to swim here, and we believed him, which made swimming here more exciting, though no one ever gave us a second thought.

We had never before stopped at the natural beach on our way to the crowded beaches of Brigantine, though we had seen it as we pedaled by. You'd get a quick glimpse of the birds-only beach through the dunes. It must have popped into Frankie mind that this would be a good fishing spot when he found the net.

Somewhere on Heron Road, Frankie swerved his bike to the shoulder and dismounted by a sand dune that rose to the sky. "Here it is," he said, pointing at the dune. "There're fish in the water behind these dunes."

CJ and I stopped behind Frankie, but Whitey stayed on his bike and circled.

"Why here?" asked CJ. "Why not where there's no dune to climb?"

"This is where the fish are. I know it. Besides, no one will be able to see us from the road, and we won't get chased."

CJ sighed. Whitey continued to circle. "I thought we were going to Brigantine," he said, circling close.

"We can't use the net on the regular Brigantine beaches," said Frankie.

"How do you know?" Whitey called as his circle brought him to the other side of the road.

"I read it on that sign back there," Frankie shouted back.

We had passed a sign that listed the regulations for proper behavior in Brigantine. It had more *Thou shalt nots* than The Ten Commandments.

"You actually read that sign?" Whitey circled close. "Nobody reads those signs."

"I do," said Frank.

CJ combed his hair and rolled his eyes. "Let's just get it over with," he said.

I was curious about the deserted beach. I liked the looks of the calm water I'd glimpsed as we were pedaling over the bridge, so I was all for following Frankie. "C'mon Whitey," I said.

Whitey circled close again. "I don't like it."

Frankie got angry. "Will you just get off your bike and come on, Whitey. Nobody's gonna see us. I've never seen you chicken out of something like this before."

We all stood by our bikes and looked at Whitey. Reluctantly, he pulled over and joined us. "I'm no chicken," he said. "I just don't think we belong here. " But he followed us when we left our bikes by the side of the road and began to climb.

On the way up, CJ fell behind. He clawed at the dune, complaining that his hair was getting ruined and his shoes were full of sand. When we reached the top, we sat on the crest of the dune and laughed at CJ as he struggled, jabbing his Cuban heels into sand. "God damn you, Frankie!" he said. "What the hell is net fishing, anyway? You're not going to catch anything!" Frankie mimicked him with a high voice. We laughed, and CJ finally scuttled his way to the top, breathing heavily.

From the top of the dune we could see the lay of the land. It was a clear day. Before us stretched a wide beach dotted with patches of "prickle-grass." At the water's edge, the calm bay lapped the shore, and a flock of sprightly sandpipers ran back and forth. Way down the beach to our right, tall cattails grew at the start of an archipelago of marsh islands. On the beach to the left stood the only sign of civilization—a surveyor's level on a tripod standing unmanned near a chunk of cut granite.

Frankie grabbed the net from me and, slinging it over his shoulder, ran straight toward the water. We followed. It was so quiet, the sand squeaking beneath our feet sounded loud. There was an eeriness about it, like we were the first people ever to set foot here.

When we got to the flats, Frankie threw the net off his shoulder and it fell in a tangled mess. We looked at Frankie for instructions. He hesitated, trying not to look perplexed.

CJ, sitting on the beach watching us—obviously not going in the water—said, "Well, Frankie, you know so much about net fishing. What now?" He lit up a cigarette.

Frank started to dance around the net, fiddling with each corner until Whitey pushed Frankie's aside and took charge. He supervised the detangling. When the net was flat, it stretched about twenty feet. Whitey said, "Frank, take your end out as far as you can. I'll stay in close and hold the other end. Richie, you walk in the middle and make sure it stays deep. We'll sweep right across." He didn't bother giving CJ an assignment.

Frankie took his end out about forty feet where the water was still only chest-high. Whitey stayed in the shallow water, bending to keep the net low. I had the best job. Midway, submerged to my hips, I guided the net while they did all the pulling. The water was cool, and the sun was hot on my shoulders.

As we dragged the net across the surf, I swore we weren't catching anything. There seemed to be no activity in the net. I thought CJ would have the last laugh. I scanned the beach for CJ and saw he was no longer alone. A short square man in a khaki uniform had joined him. They were watching us with interest. I could almost hear CJ telling the man that we were wasting our time. They were having a laugh and a smoke. I presumed he was the surveyor.

As we finished our sweep, I felt some fluttering in the net. Frankie circled in close, and we tugged the net toward the beach, moving as fast as we could. Lifting the net out of the shallow water, we could see that we had a good haul. The net was teeming with life. We laughed out loud and ran our catch to the flat sand. When we laid the net out and looked at the profusion that it held, we were speechless. The surveyor joined us. The net seemed to contain a miniature version of every sea creature I had ever seen around Atlantic City—and plenty I had never seen. Flapping around were tiny blowfish and sea robins, silversides so tiny you could hardly see them, baby kingfish, a few flounder the size of silver dollars, and a rockfish no bigger than a minnow. There were some other kinds of fish I couldn't name—and every one a baby. Escaping in all directions from the net were calico crabs, blue pincers, spider crabs, and rock crabs—all tiny versions of the ones we routinely saw between the rock piles in AC. Different kinds of worms squirmed through brown seaweed, along with some ugly underwater bugs. A hundred tiny jellyfish sparkled in the confusion. There were two little starfish, too. But in the midst of all these, one fish really stood out. It looked like a dolphin—not a porpoise, which we sometimes called a dolphin—but one of those square-headed tropical fish that grow to an enormous size and have a rainbow coat. It was covered with gleaming iridescent scales and dark black spots, and it was almost all head. I'd never seen a fish like that before. As it jerked helplessly in the middle of the pile, a little bigger than all the other fish, we gazed at it as though we were waiting for it to say something.

Whitey's trance was the first to break. He fell to his knees and grabbed the beautiful rainbow fish out of the teeming net. Without a word, he ran the fish back to the water and set it free in the shallows.

"Whudja do that for?" Frankie asked Whitey when he returned. "That fish mighta been big enough to eat. Rita mighta cooked it."

Whitey glared at him.

"I guess we ought to throw them back," Frankie said. "They're too small. But I want to keep a few to show Rita." He knelt to gather the tiny flounder.

"Leave it be," said Whitey. "This is a spawning ground."

Frankie looked up, surprised, like Whitey had no business knowing words like "spawning." "A what?"

"A place where—"

"Oh, fuck you. Just this one."

Whitey knelt next to Frank and, grabbing his wrist, said, "Leave it be, I said. Leave it be, or I'll tell about the net."

"But..." Frankie rose without the fish.

Whitey and I each took an end of the net and dragged it back to the water. Frankie joined us reluctantly pretending to help. We overturned the net and shook out all the babies. Whitey untangled a few crabs that were ensnared. Frankie tried to pocket a starfish, but

Whitey caught him. We freed all the creatures that hadn't escaped on their own.

When we returned, the surveyor was talking to CJ. Hat in one hand, he ran his other hand through his silver hair and said, "I was just telling your buddy here, how that was the prettiest fish I ever saw, and I've been living around here for forty years." Then he started back to his tripod.

The sun was beginning to descend, deepening the colors of the bay. Soon the sky would be green, and the water blue. Time to go home. Frankie and I had baked to an even deeper copper color. CJ's nose was cherry red. But Whitey remained as white as the belly of a blowfish.

As we folded the net, CJ watched and said, "While you were fishing, that surveyor told me this is a restricted beach. We aren't allowed here."

"So what?" said Frankie.

"You know what else he told me?" CJ made a sweeping motion with his hand. "He said this whole area is going to be filled in, with concrete and junk, so they can build a marina and a shopping center."

"Really?" said Frankie. "That's pretty neat. I wonder what kind of stores they'll have."

"It's bad," said Whitey. "It's bad. Once they fill it in there won't be any place for the fish!"

"Maybe they'll keep a part natural," I offered. I looked around. "I like this spot. We should come back."

Frankie gave Whitey a nudge. "Whaddaya say we take your dad's boat out one of these days and try to find this beach again by coming in through the bay?"

CJ said, "Oh, God."

"I told you before, Frankie, unless my dad is there, I can't use that boat."

"You have a boat, Whitey?" I liked the idea.

"Aw, he'd never know the difference," said Frankie. He held the wet net out for CJ to carry home. CJ said he didn't want to do it, but Frankie said something in his ear, and CJ relented. He gave Frankie a poisonous look before he took the net and slung it over his shoulder.

On the way home, Frankie badgered Whitey about the boat. I was tired and began to have misgivings about the day. Whitey was right. We shouldn't have gone there. We didn't belong. It was a place for little creatures. We'd thrown them back, but they were just babies, and we'd most likely frightened them. Also, we had trespassed on a restricted area, broken the law. Suppose we'd gotten caught? And it was a shame that the pretty beach was doomed. All those sandpipers would have to find a new home. Worst of all, I felt guilty and afraid my mom might find out where I'd been all day. I was excited at the beginning of the trip, but now I felt lousy, and I hoped Whitey would outlast Frankie's relentless pressure to steal his dad's boat.

2.
The Song of the Wandering Aengus

YOU CAN *depend on the beach not to change. You may go to a different beach. But the scene doesn't change. Only the faces change. There's the group of neighbors in a semi-circle, jabbering away. There's the family, with mom slathering the kids with lotion. The lifeguards are talking to a pretty girl.... The beach is the beach.*

I brought an unlikely beach read with me, an anthology of poetry entitled Twice-Read Poems. *It's a collection of well-known poems by British and American poets. I need to choose a dozen or so poems from this book because I agreed to teach a class in poetry this fall at a nearby for-profit college.* Twice-Read Poems *is the official text. A guy who lives in my building is an administrator in this school and he offered me the job to teach Appreciating Poetry for one semester because the regular instructor is ill. He knows that I'm a retired English teacher, and he was in a hurry to find someone to fill in, so he knocked on my door. Although this college specializes in information technology, the students are required to take a few humanities courses. We'll see how enthusiastic computer geeks are about poetry.*

I can see how this school makes a profit; they're paying me beans. But I'm always looking for things to do in retirement—things that will keep the old brain working. So I'm hunting through Twice-Read Poems *for some verses that might appeal to the IT set.*

I've just read "The Song of the Wandering Aengus," by W.B. Yeats, and I think it'll make the cut. It's narrated by an old transient, who is fishing for his dinner at a stream in the woods, and he catches a magic fish. The fish transforms into a "glimmering girl," who runs off, but not before she calls his name. So he pursues her and declares that he will pursue her forever.

I'm thinking the boys (I'm assuming my computer geeks will be boys) will respond to the idea of a fish transforming into a glimmering girl. First, there's the element of fantasy, a popular genre, and then there's the element of sex. I'll point out that when the girl runs into the woods, she's most likely naked, since she was just a fish. They'll understand that when the girl calls the name of the old guy, she's seducing him. Then I'll push them toward the theme of the poem, which is that we should pursue beauty and passion until the very end of our lives and never give up. The sexy imagery will be the hook.

If these college-age kids are anything like the students I taught in high school, they'll look at the poem in a more literal way. They'll see the narrator as an old homeless guy stalking a young woman. They'll go for the jugular and think I chose the poem because I am a dirty old man who identifies with the perverted narrator. So I'll have to insist that the poem operates on a symbolic level—that the girl is not a real girl, but a symbol of beauty. Aengus is not a bum, but everyman— every old man, anyway. And the theme is an uplifting theme—not at all perverse—exhorting us never to submit to the ravages of time.

Besides all this, it's a charming poem, with a catchy tempo and a soaring crescendo that culminates in an inspirational climax. It's a song, and it should be irresistible.

As for me, I think old age is a lot more prosaic. Age is about loss— and accepting loss—not about the pursuit of beauty. As my dentist likes to say as he gauges how much my gums have receded since he last checked: "You don't get long in the tooth. You get short in the gums." Age attenuates everything. You literally shrink. In an effort to stave off the atrophy of my muscles, I added weight-lifting to my exercise routine. Formerly, all I needed to stay in shape was a long walk once a day. But I noticed that every part of me except my legs was getting flabby. So I started lifting weights three times a week. But, after months of pumping iron, when I looked in the mirror, I couldn't see any difference. Apparently my muscles were atrophying as fast as I was building them up—a zero-sum game. It's all a matter of time before my muscles start wasting away faster than I can build them up. Soon, I'll be too old and too tired to do enough exercise to offset the atrophy. Flab is our fate.

Mortality enters into my every decision. Last month, I replaced my fourteen-year-old Subaru with a new one, even though the old car was still in good condition. I reckoned if I waited to buy a new car, I'd buy it too close to the time of my demise, cheating myself out of time to enjoy it. It's now or never, I thought. I drive as little as possible, and I like not driving, so the old car may have lasted for the duration, but I figured if I liked not driving my old car, I would really like not driving a new one. Now that I have a new car, there's a chance I will live long enough to not drive it for long enough so I feel like I've gotten as much out of it as I could.

You get old, and you lose everything that once was pleasurable. My wife died a few years ago, so I lost access to the tenderness of a woman. And I don't feel inclined to replace her. I've lost the desire. All of my close friends, by a kind of perfect storm, have disappeared, either by dying or moving away, leaving me pretty much alone, with only a few acquaintances. I had to give up drinking because, instead of making me feel better, even a little bit of booze gave me a headache. Life is boring without alcohol. Caffeine too, nowadays, muffles my brain instead of cranking it up. Coffee and tea, dependable old friends, have turned on me. And it's no fun to wake up without them. I can't eat risky foods either—all the good stuff. My diet is bland. I'm on the verge of vegetarianism. You're condemned to a healthy diet when you age. I read the other day that I should not be eating more than one tablespoon of butter a week if I plan to survive. So the whole wheat toast I ate for breakfast this morning had so little butter on it it may as well have had none at all; it was just a dot of token butter.

I stay at home now, most of the time. Just me and my radio....

I could take up religion, I suppose, as a respite from my losses, though it seems a little late for that. I've denied the existence of God all of my life. I've always wondered why anyone would bother with the fanciful notion of spirituality in what is obviously a material world. I could never convince myself that faith is the answer—to anything. Even at my weekly yoga class, when the instructor directs us to put our two hands together, prayer-like, "at heart's center," and bow our heads, I don't do it. I feel silly doing anything remotely religious. Religion poses a stubborn paradox. It offers comfort, but to receive it you have to believe in a lie.

Old Aengus managed to convince himself that if he persists in the pursuit of magic girls and golden apples he will cheat time and remain vital. Maybe he's right. Maybe I ought to find some passion— some religious or romantic quest—and talk myself into its virtue and pursue it, regardless of its validity. Would it be worth the effort to *pursue a lie? No, I think Aengus should just adjust to his old age and relax. Chasing girls—symbolic or real—at his age—is a fool's errand. Adjust, Aengus, adjust. Accept what you have lost. Are you nuts? Chasing girls all over Creation at your age....*

In any event, this poem should give us something to talk about. Even if I have trouble suspending disbelief in metaphysical matters, and I might have difficulty pushing Aengus's point about pursuing passion, in their youth and naiveté my students might buy his conclusions without much convincing.

•

WHEN we were rolling home from Brigantine on Maryland Avenue, we heard a loud hubbub behind us. Someone shouted, "Hold up, bitches!" I was taking up the rear of our file, and when I turned around to see who was calling, I saw a group of five or six black kids on bikes, about our age, gaining on us. We were riding on the North Side, above Atlantic Avenue and this was Black turf. Frankie, CJ, and Whitey had also turned around and seen our pursuers and, as if on cue, we all hauled ass. So the race was on. We had left the wetlands of the back bay by this time and were in Atlantic City proper, amid rush-hour traffic, so we were confined to riding on the shoulder of the road, single file. All we could do was try to outrun these guys, who were whooping it up back there, knowing they outnumbered us and had home-court advantage. I foresaw a confrontation that wouldn't end well for us so, though drained from the long day in the sun, I felt energized and pedaled with all I had.

Most likely they would not cross Atlantic Avenue, a few blocks away, which was the dividing line between the white and black sections of town. So we made for Atlantic. But they were fast—and loud. They gained on us. When they just about caught up, I braced myself, expecting to be pushed off my bike at high speed. Two guys squeezed in beside us and I ducked, waiting to get whacked. But they passed me by. Instead, they pulled up alongside Frankie and Whitey. There was some trash-talking. Then, all at once, we stopped. Frankie and their head guy dismounted, walked onto the median and, for fifteen seconds, engaged in a hectic fight, Frankie punching wildly at the air like a kangaroo, and the black kid bobbing and weaving like a boxer. The rest of us pulled our bikes onto the median and watched.

I stared in disbelief, but all the others—white and black—rooted and heckled. And then, just as quickly as it had started, the fight stopped, as though someone rang a bell to end the round. Frankie and his adversary remounted their bikes, as did the rest of us, and we rode together like one gang for a block. Frankie's opponent said he was "still a fucking turkey," and Frankie responded by challenging him to a bike race "anywhere, any time." I heard Whitey's counterpart call him "Whitey-White" and Whitey respond by calling him "Spook." CJ and I got off with nothing but disdainful looks—especially CJ, on account of his pink bike. Then, our pursuers turned off at the next street and left us alone.

I pedaled up to Frankie. "Who were those guys?"

"Who, Eggy and Spook? Shitheads from school."

"Eggy?"

"Yeah, well, it's actually Egg Head, but you say it Egg-*ee*. I think his real name is Clarence. Look at his head."

I spotted Clarence, leading his troop, pedaling onto Arctic Avenue, and the nickname Egg Head was appropriate.

"Why the fight?"

"We always do that. We've been doing it since the third grade. He's such a jerk!"

"They scared the hell out of me," I said.

"Clarence and Spook? They're OK, I guess—for assholes. Don't you have colored people in Philly?"

"Well, yeah, but they're a little less friendly when they fight. Why didn't they know CJ?"

"CJ! He dropped out of school years ago."

"What, when he was ten?"

I noticed a tiny dead flounder peeking from the pocket of Frankie's swim trunks. Rigor mortis had set in. The roughhouse must have brought it up.

Home, I parked my bike in the yard behind our apartment and chained it to a post. I always chained the bike when I left it in the yard, although I rarely chained it anywhere else. This way my mother, who always saw the bike chained, would not accuse me of negligence if the bike were stolen. As far as she could tell, it was always chained. If it were stolen, which was unlikely, I'd say someone must have cut the chain. So the bike was chained in its safest location, the backyard, and it went unchained where it might be stolen—everywhere else. Mom's nagging was worse than my worries about the security of the bike.

To enter our apartment, the basement apartment, we used the back door, which opened into the kitchen. As I entered, I swung the door wide open and let it close behind me with a bang. It was a wooden screen door with a good spring, so it closed with a terrific noise. I loved that sound, although it irritated everyone else.

"How many times have I told you not to bang that door!" Mom said from her station at the stove.

"Oops."

I sat in my place and said nothing. A good way to keep out of trouble was to keep quiet and avoid questions. Going to Brigantine with my friends was a clear violation of my mother's beach rules—a violation major enough to sentence me to sit on the beach with her and Harry for a while if she found out—so I kept my mouth shut and my head down. I thought of some excuses I might make if Mom somehow found out I wasn't on the beach; if, let's say, Harry had wandered over to where my friends and I sat on New Hampshire Avenue beach and hadn't seen me; or if someone on New Hampshire beach had almost drowned, so the lifeguards had to row out and save him, causing a commotion, and I didn't know anything about it. I prepared some whoppers.

I smelled trouble. Mom and Harry were concentrating on what they were doing and not talking to me. My mother was holding her trusty spatula, fussing around the stove, and Harry was sitting across from me, poring over the box scores in the sports section of *The Philadelphia Inquirer*. He could quote statistics about most of the players in the National League, and his knowledge of the Phillies was flawless. I sensed that Mom and Harry were getting ready to pounce.

I grabbed a twisted roll from a plate on the table and broke the silence. "How are the Phils doing, Har?" I asked.

"In the basement, as usual," said Harry, continuing his study.

Harry had the look of a scholar. He wore his thick tortoise shell glasses all the time, even when he showered, and he wore shoes and socks to the beach. He never learned the essentials of childhood fun— spitting, whistling, riding a two-wheeler, and lying to your mother. He liked to watch TV, sit on the beach with Mom and her lady friends, and memorize trivia. He knew the specifications of every car in the General Motors exhibit at the entrance to the Steel Pier.

"Well, we're in the basement, too," I joked. "The basement apartment." Nobody laughed.

"So, where were you going on your bike when I saw you this morning?" Harry asked.

Mom put a plate with three lamb chops, a scoop of mashed potatoes, and some peas before me. I was starving and dug in. There was no better way to stay out of trouble than to praise Mom's cooking. "Mmmm, my favorite," I said.

Mom scowled at me, folding her arms, spatula still in hand, and waited for me to answer Harry's question.

I looked at Mom then Harry. "Nowhere, just a ride."

Mom was skeptical. "Where exactly is 'nowhere'?"

"Am I in trouble or something?" I mixed my lamb pieces with potato and scooped it into my mouth.

Mom went back to the sink and turned on the tap. "Around what time did you see Richie?" she asked Harry.

"Around 12:00," said Harry. "He was riding toward the golf course. Probably looking for beaches without lifeguards."

I took advantage of the opportunity to tell some truth. "I wasn't looking for beaches without lifeguards. I was just riding."

"Riding where, buddy-boy?" asked Mom.

"Nowhere," I repeated, preparing another lamb and potato combination.

Harry continued the interrogation. "Were you going surfing with Frankie Talone by any chance?" Harry looked toward Mom then me. "Frankie told me that he had a surfboard, and he asked me if I wanted to go surfing at States Avenue, where there are no lifeguards."

"Frankie? Asked *you*? To go surfing?" I laughed.

"Well," said Mom, turning and wagging her spatula at me, "were you surfing? Frankie can do what he wants, but you will not get on a surfboard! Never, d'you hear? Surfboard! You could get killed. Why would you do such a thing? No lifeguards? You'll be sorry for hanging around with those bums. Wait and see. "

"Wait and see-ee," repeated Harry.

Their suspicion that I was surfing revealed that Mom and Harry had no clue about my actual whereabouts, which was a relief. I wondered if Frankie really had a surfboard, though. If so, he hadn't told me.

"Harry's nuts, Mom," I said with my mouth full. "When he saw me I was on my way to the Boardwalk Motel to buy a Coke. Then I came right back by way of the avenue." My mother and Harry were quiet, which was good. It meant they had nothing more. I tightened my alibi. "Me and Frankie and Whitey were swimming all day on New Hampshire beach, just like usual." My mother did not know CJ, so I left his name out to avoid further questions.

"Where'd you get the money for the Coke?" Harry asked.

"We collected bottles on the beach for deposit."

Luckily, at this point in the interrogation, my other brother Fred walked in. He was miserable, as usual. "Hate, hate, hate..." he muttered under his breath as he eased the screen door shut. Fred was three years older than Harry, and he was enduring his first summer of full-time employment. He worked in a souvenir shop in front of the Breakers Hotel. "Hate, hate, hate..." he said, peeling off his sport jacket and hanging it on the back of his chair. He'd already loosened his tie. I took advantage of the distraction to make some headway with my chops.

Fred had a predictable routine when he came home from work. He stepped through the door, quietly grumbling *"Hate, hate, hate..."* until someone asked what was bothering him and gave him an opportunity to vent. At the beginning of the summer, my mother came right out and said, "What's the matter, Fred?" But Fred let loose with such terrible stories about how sadistic his boss was, and he told these stories in such a desperate tone, that he disturbed everyone, especially Mom, who felt guilty that Fred was not having a proper summer vacation. So we became cautious. We didn't prompt Fred. We hoped he would just grumble until he felt pacified and spare us the details. If Mom quickly slung a dinner he liked in front of him the chances were good that he'd keep quiet. And Fred liked the looks of his chops when they arrived.

Fred's problem was that he was an avid fisherman, had been for many summers, and now he was stuck at work all day while schools of catchable fish were swimming back and forth in the ocean just a stone's throw from where he worked on the boardwalk. Almost every night, after dinner, Fred jumped into his hip waders and rushed out to join his buddies for a few hours of fishing in the surf, which would put him at ease—although these abbreviated sessions were no substitute for the all-day excursions of his previous summers.

"Hate, hate, hate..."

I decided Fred's ravings might serve as a good cover for me, so I gave him his prompt. "So, Fred," I asked, "how was your day at the office?"

Harry and Mom winced.

"On the last day of the summer, I'm going to murder that son-of-a-bitch," said Fred. "Today was the worst. I thought he was just going to make me stand out on the boardwalk as usual and shout *'Toys! Gifts! Souvenirs!'* But no. Since it was so hot today, he decided it would be a good idea for me to clean all the stuff in the window. So I spent the day crawling around in the front window where it was about 200 degrees, cleaning every trinket, while that maniac watched me to make sure I put everything back exactly where it was. Hate! Hate! HATE!"

Fred was on a tear. I finished eating to the accompaniment of Fred's rant. "That son-of-a-bitch knew where every ashtray was. And he watched me like a hawk. Hsing Chang from next door brought me a glass of water because he felt sorry for me. I have to kill that bastard. He needs to be killed." Fred wrung an imaginary neck, then brooded as he ate.

"It's just for the summer," said Mom. "Then you're off to college. I like Hsing Chang. There's a clock I want there. Can you get a discount?"

"Maybe."

Sensing an opportunity, Harry brought the conversation back to me. "I took a walk to New Hampshire beach around 2:00," he said, "and I didn't see you or your pals."

"Aw, c'mon Harry, lay off! Am I bothering you?" I tried my best to sound indignant. Then I turned to leave the table, hoping to slip away from any further cross-examination, but Mom stood in my path, spatula in hand. "You said you were on New Hampshire Beach. Why didn't Harry see you there?" she asked.

"Did you walk as far as the Oriental Avenue Jetty?" I asked Harry.

"No."

"Well, that's why you didn't see us. We were on the rocks."

"Oy," my mother objected, "I don't want you climbing on those rocks. Remember how you got impetigo last summer."

Fred looked up. The rock pile at Oriental Avenue was a popular fishing spot. "Leave him alone, Mom," he said. "There's nothing wrong with the rocks." He turned toward me inquisitively. "Were they catching anything?"

"Some kingies," I said, "and a lot of sea robins." This was a safe bet since the fishermen on the jetty always caught these.

"Well," said Fred, "I'm gonna hit the surf after dinner. Tomorrow, instead of *toys, gifts, and souvenirs!* I'm going to holler *junk, schlock, and mouse turds!* See if I don't."

"I'm finished, Ma. Can I go to my room and lay down for a while?" I gave Harry a parting dirty look and headed for my room.

As I fled, Mom asked, "What are you doing tonight?"

"I don't know." I shut my door.

I heard Mom say, "Take a shower before you get into bed!" but I didn't listen. The wind had blown the sand off me on my ride home from Brigantine, and I was clean enough.

In bed, I read a few pages of a comic. Superman had married Lana Lang and they had two super-kids. But I was too sleepy to read. I stared at the silver flowers on the ceiling wallpaper. Softly, the evening slipped into night. Some tourists clicked by my window chatting hopefully as they headed for the boardwalk. Somewhere Big Ned was being congratulated for winning another game, perhaps striking out twenty-seven guys in a row. Frankie was telling his Aunt Rita about his fishing expedition to Brigantine—showing her the little dead flounder. Whitey would be warming a can of chili for his little brother if their father wasn't home. And CJ and his many sisters would be fighting over the TV. I tried to come up with the names of CJ's sisters: Theresa, Angela, Marie.... I could hear Fred in the next room gearing up for surf-fishing. With squeaks and thuds, he lumbered past my door in hip waders. He went out the back door, dreams of huge rockfish swimming in his head. I wondered what my father did all week in Philadelphia as he waited for the weekend when he would join us down the shore. Just worked and slept, I guessed. That was all he ever did.

Down the hall, my brother Harry was playing his favorite game: Lying in bed, throwing a ball up in the air, and catching it, all the while announcing an imaginary baseball game using National League line-ups. "And Schoendienst strikes out!" I heard him tell his listeners. The Phils were playing a night game with the Braves in Harry's mind.

Mom was knitting in the front room, worried about my oldest brother Albert, who wandered the world.

Far away, a sad seagull shrieked.

I thought of Theresa and her bruised back. I fantasized that it was

Marie, not Theresa, who ironed naked. She turned around and I saw her breasts, which were the breasts of Busty Russell. I scaled them down to a proportional size and removed the silver pasties. She leaned her elbows back against the ironing board.... I fell asleep.

I dreamed we were back at the bay, dragging the net across the shallows. The afternoon stood still. Suddenly, I felt something big struggling in the net. We could only see its shadow under the surface of the water, but it wound and dove like a giant eel. We encircled it in the net. A cloud moved a dark shadow over the bay. We hauled our catch out of the surf and onto the flat sand. Opening the net, we discovered a fat striped bass. Whitey looked up and asked, "Is it pregnant?"

My brother Harry's voice broke into the dream. He was on his way to the bathroom. "Richie fell asleep without taking a shower," he sang, but it only woke me for a moment.

I SLEPT ten hours. Sun and sea are powerful narcotics. I was awakened in the morning by someone scratching the screen of my window and whispering my name: *"Rich-ie, Rich-ie."* My room looked out on a driveway, and anyone who cared to could look through my screened window and see me in bed, though no one ever did.

"Who's there?" I asked softly, although I recognized the voice. I peeked up and saw Frankie. He was drinking a grapefruit soda from a bottle.

"It's Frank," he whispered. "C'mon out. I got a surprise for you."

I looked at the clock on the wall. It was almost five-thirty. The sun was not up. "Whatta ya want, Frank? It's awful early."

"Just come on out," insisted Frankie.

"I gotta eat breakfast and stuff."

"OK," said Frank, "I'll meet you at six o'clock in front of my house. And wear your swim trunks, because we might be going in the water—*if our luck runs out.*" With this riddle he disappeared down the drive like a cat.

My mother began her days before dawn. She was already in the kitchen eating oatmeal when I appeared. "You were asleep by seven o'clock last night," she said. "You must have had a busy day yesterday. Go take a shower and I'll make you breakfast. What do you want?"

"Got any bacon?"

"I think so."

"I'll have bacon and eggs with toasted raisin bread," I said.

In the shower, I wondered what Frankie meant by going in the water if we were *not lucky*. This could mean anything. Maybe we were going to do some rock climbing on a new jetty he'd discovered. Or maybe he'd finally found the way to sneak onto the Steel Pier by climbing up the side.

At the kitchen table, I could hear the sounds of the city awakening. The beach cleaning tractor groaned in the distance and, echoing up our driveway, I heard the voices of some cyclists heading for the boards. As I ate breakfast, my mother invited me to spend the day with Harry and her on the beach. "What's the matter with Vermont Beach?" she asked. "It's going to be a beautiful day. You can just as easily swim on our beach as anywhere else. You and your brother can have a game of cards—"

The thought made me shudder. "I have plans," I said.

Hmmm, I thought, what should I tell Mom I'm doing today? Something permissible that would take up considerable time, just in case. "Me and Frankie are going to take a walk to Captain Starns to see the porpoises."

"They have porpoises there?"

"Yeah, they keep them in a kind of pen, built right in the ocean—surrounded by a dock. They swim back and forth all day." As a consolation, I added, "Maybe we'll go swimming with you on Vermont beach afterwards."

We heard someone walking sprightly up our drive.

"That must be Izzy," said Mom. "He's going to fix the sink in the back room."

Izzy was Mr. Goldfarb of Goldfarb's Guest House, located directly across the street from Whitey's place. It was his grandchildren I'd seen at the miniature golf course the day before. Izzy could fix anything. He was a one-man contracting crew. He had converted the rooms on the second and third floors of our house into separate apartments. He was, in my mother's words, "as strong as iron." His identification number from Buchenwald, the concentration camp he'd survived, was tattooed on his wrist.

Izzy knocked on the back door. "Vot's dat I schmell," he asked. "Pik? Are you eating pik in dere?" He eyed us through the screen door. He was no taller than me and had only two teeth.

My mother smiled at me as I popped a bit of bacon into my mouth.

"Come on in, Izzy," she said.

"You feed da *kinder* pik?" He entered, shaking his head. "Tsk, tsk. Are you a Jew?"

"Well, Izzy," said Mom, "you know how it is. We're Jewish, but we eat pork. So how are you?" My mother smiled at Izzy and ushered him in.

"Ach!" he said, "Vat's da use a' complainink? Mine daughter vants me to moof in mit her by Cherry Hill," He waved away his troubles. "But vot's da trouble mit da sink?" he asked.

"It's leaking," said Mom. "Underneath. The sink next to the washer. Come on back and take a look." She led Izzy toward the back room where the washing machine was.

"I'm leaving, Mom," I called as they disappeared.

"Will you be back for lunch?" Mom asked.

But I was out the door, letting it swing closed with a bang. "Vot de hell vas dat?" said Izzy. "I can schtop dat noise mit a door damper...."

In front of Frankie's place, CJ and Whitey's little brother Chip were sitting on the steps. Chip looked like a miniature version of Whitey. Same round pink face, same pure white crew cut, same blue eyes. But Chip wasn't bright like Whitey. Frankie told me that Whitey's mom had fallen down some steps while she was pregnant with Chip, and that was why he was a little slow. Mouth open, he looked back and forth at me and CJ as we talked.

"Where's Frankie?" I asked.

"He claims he's got a cooler full of sodas and sandwiches," CJ explained with a yawn, "and he's inside getting them." CJ fixed his DA, tapping the front to fix the curl, then blowing upwards to get it just right.

"So what's going on? Why did Frankie wake me up?"

"Oh, you weren't here last night, were you?"

"I fell asleep."

"Well, do you remember back in Brigantine yesterday how Frankie kept bothering Whitey about his father's boat?"

"Yeah."

"Well, we were hanging around up at Big Ned's place last night after his game, and Frankie wouldn't let Whitey alone about that boat. He kept saying, 'You ain't really even got no boat.' And Whitey kept saying 'Wanna bet?' And Frankie said, 'I'll bet you anything.' Whitey was getting pretty mad, but Frankie wouldn't stop pestering him.

Finally Whitey gave in and said that he would take us all out for a ride in his father's boat in the morning to prove that he had one. But he said if he did, Frankie would have to bring us all lunch. That was the deal. So Frankie said, 'I ain't worried about bringing nobody no lunch, because you ain't got no boat.' And Whitey just said, 'You be on Vermont Beach around six-thirty tomorrow morning, and I'll show you who doesn't have a boat!'"

"So Whitey is off getting his dad's boat?"

"Yup."

"And we're going to set out at 6:30?"

"Yup."

I had mixed feelings, but I said, "That's...great!"

Whitey's little brother smiled a crooked smile. One of his eyeballs quivered.

"The only problem is Whitey's not allowed to use the boat without his dad knowing. That's how this little snot got to come along." CJ cocked a thumb toward Chip who lost his smile and reddened. "Snotty here said he'd tell on Whitey if Whitey didn't take him."

"Up your ass!" said Chip.

"Is it a speedboat? How big is it?" I asked. I was glad that I'd given my mother an all-day excuse. "How about Ned?"

"He couldn't come. He's got baseball practice." CJ took a small mirror from his shirt pocket and checked his teeth and the curl in his hair. I considered how totally wrong his tight jeans and pointy shoes were for this occasion.

Just then Frankie came down his steps toting a large cooler with Wasserman's Meat Market stenciled on the side. He set it on the pavement where he proudly popped the lid and invited our inspection. It contained a half-dozen Canada Dry grapefruit sodas and a jumble of peanut butter and jelly sandwiches badly wrapped in wax paper.

"It took me most of the morning to get this stuff together," he said. "Let's go."

We took turns hauling the cooler down the street to the beach. There, we sat on the sand next to the Vermont Avenue jetty where Whitey had promised to land. To our left, the sun changed from a copper disk to a white fire as it climbed into the sky. We shared a grapefruit soda and waited.

"So where'd you get the cooler?" CJ asked Frankie.

"I borrowed it from old Wasserman, your neighbor. He

won't mind."

CJ chuckled. "Was that Wasserman's net we used yesterday?"

"Why would Wasserman need a net?"

"What kind of boat is it?" I asked.

"A skiff," said Frank, "about as long as that lifeguard boat there." He pointed to the lifeguard's boat on the beach which, at this hour, was turned upside-down and rested on its rollers.

The plan was for Whitey to wake up at four o'clock and take a jitney to the harbor behind Captain Starns, where his dad moored the boat. He'd commander the boat and steer it from Starns through the bay and into the ocean. He'd curl around the Oriental Avenue jetty and pull into the surf at Vermont Avenue, where he would meet us. We would pull the boat onto the beach, climb in, and embark. Then we'd head back toward the bay to search for the empty beach we had visited the day before, to see if we could find it by water.

The bay area, back by Starns, would not be treacherous for Whitey. It was calm. But, in a skiff the size of a lifeguard boat, when he reached the ocean, it would be more dangerous. And by the time he reached the Oriental Avenue jetty he'd be traveling through rough waters and strong currents. Fortunately, Vermont Avenue was only two blocks from the Oriental Avenue jetty, so he would not have to deal with the most treacherous leg for long. But the choppy ocean part, especially around the jetty and onto the beach, would require skill. Then we'd have to repeat the journey in reverse, with a boatload of kids, on our way back to the bay.

We waited, facing the surf. The ocean was pretty calm, but Whitey was late.

"He ain't coming," Frankie said, reaching into the cooler for another grapefruit soda.

"Up your ass," said Chip.

"What made you buy grapefruit soda?" asked CJ, looking at the bottle and sneering.

"That's all they had," said Frankie. CJ rolled his eyes.

The longer we waited, staring at the ocean, the more nervous I became. I wondered if there'd be life jackets on Whitey's boat. I'd been in this kind of small craft before, fishing with my brother and his friends, and they were strict about life jackets. I didn't want to bring up the subject and seem like a sissy, but I hoped we'd have some life jackets, if only for little Chip, who was now engrossed in scratching open a mosquito bite on his shin.

In the midst of my worries, I heard a motor working overtime. We looked up. A green skiff with a small outboard motor popped out from behind the Oriental Avenue jetty. "I think that's Captain Whitey!" I said, pointing seaward. And sure enough he had rounded the jetty and was heading toward us at a crisp clip.

Whitey was seated in the stern of the craft with his hand on the tiller. The bow skipped through the little waves, splashing with each bounce. We waved our arms and shouted. Spotting us, Whitey raised a fist in triumph.

When he was close enough, we ran into the water and dragged the boat ashore. Not CJ, of course, who didn't want to ruin his rat-stabber shoes. Amid our noisy congratulations and back-slaps, Whitey stopped the outboard and tilted it up.

"Toldja," said Chip, looking sideways at nothing.

The skiff was about fifteen feet long, with plank seats. The outboard was the smallest I'd ever seen. She leaked a little, and there were no life jackets, not even a ring buoy. But we were raring to go, so we stowed our gear amidship and hopped on board.

Heading out to sea. I could tell from the concerned look on Whitey's face that he hadn't realized the weight he was taking aboard. The outboard motor groaned painfully, and the boat drooped in the water until its rail was no more than ten inches above the surface.

But the ocean was calm, and Whitey seemed to know what he was doing. So it wasn't until we were well out to sea that we lapsed into a fearful silence.

"Hey, Whitey," I asked, looking at the distant shore, "shouldn't we have life jackets?"

Frankie and Chip looked at me and snorted. They shook their heads with disapproval.

"My dad's got them in the trunk of his car, I think," said Whitey.

I almost said, *"Lot of good..."* but I bit my tongue. Instead, reaching over the rail and easily touching the water, I asked, "What'll we do if she tips over?"

Frankie and Chip looked at me again and guffawed with disapproval. But I noticed that CJ, who sat next to me, wasn't laughing. Pale and shaking, he gripped his plank seat with both hands.

"If she capsizes, we'll all meet underneath the boat," said Whitey. "There'll be plenty of air under the boat, and we can hang on the benches and decide what to do next."

I looked at the deep churning sea we crawled through and considered how much pleasure it had given me all my life, bearing me up so nicely as I swam through the surf, always gentle and accommodating; and now it was transformed into a fearsome thing, swirling around and bobbing up too high for comfort, ready to do mischief. As we rounded the Oriental Avenue jetty—the most dangerous part of the journey—the choppy water slammed against the sides of the skiff, and some water splashed over the rails and gathered at the bottom of the boat. Just to our side, we could see the ocean crashing into the jetty and then sucking backwards, ebbing and flowing crazily through the rocks.

I thought, Harry and Mom were right! Safe is good, risk is bad.

Frankie was sitting in the stern with Whitey and, as the motor sputtered, Frankie began pleading with Whitey to allow him to steer the boat for a while. But Whitey wouldn't hear of it. "Look," he said, "this is my dad's boat. If anything happens to it, he'll kill me. We shouldn't even be here. So lay off!"

Frank implored. "Aw, c'mon, I know how to steer this thing."

"Up your ass," said Chip, leaning forward and grabbing Frankie's arm. The boat trembled.

"Stop moving, you little snot," said CJ, pulling Chip back onto his plank.

"Lemme steer!" Frankie demanded, and he put his hand on the tiller over Whitey's hand and pulled.

This made the boat rock dangerously. The rail missed touching the surface of the water by less than an inch. CJ squeezed my knee, and my heart jumped. Some fishermen who were fishing from the jetty pointed at us and laughed, but I couldn't see what was so funny about a bunch of kids rocking back and forth in a tiny boat arguing over who should steer.

Whitey reddened. "Get off it! Get the hell off it!" he roared, and he tried yanking the tiller away from Frankie. The boat pitched as the boys struggled. A few gallons of water came over the side as we tried to balance the boat by shifting our weight according to how she tilted.

CJ and I pleaded, "C'mon, Frank, c'mon, Frank!" and he stopped trying to pull the tiller from Whitey. But he refused to let go. The two boys glared at each other defiantly.

I tried to defuse the situation and said, "You know, Frankie, I'm sorry you didn't bring your net because we might be able to use it today. Where *did* you get that net?"

Frankie pushed the tiller away, causing the boat to shudder, but at least he let go, and we all breathed a sigh of relief. I think Frankie was glad I gave him an excuse to back off. He began to spin a yarn. "My dad left it when he took off. He left a whole room full of fishing equipment in the back of the house. He worked for a while on a fishing boat and since he was the foreman he was allowed to take stuff home."

"Oh, brother," CJ moaned. "Give me a sandwich."

"Me too," said Chip.

Frankie fished two limp sandwiches out of the cooler, unwrapped them, and shook some water off. He looked at me and pointed inside the cooler. My breakfast was sustaining me, so I said, "No thanks."

"So, is that where your dad is now, fishing on a boat?" I asked.

"Naw," Frankie said between bites. "He's in Texas. He left on a bus. I'm gonna see him this winter."

Our journey was going well now. We were cutting through the waves. The fearsome Oriental Avenue jetty was behind us, and the coastline now consisted mainly of beaches within swimming distance. Some older girls waved to us from Dewy Beach, and we waved back proudly.

We were reminiscing about the things we'd done on some of these beaches when Chip pointed over the rail and said, "Ew, what's that?"

Looking into the water, we noticed that the ocean had a reddish tint. We were in the midst of a red current that stretched for a mile like a wide ribbon under the surface. Because we were so close to the water, we could see what created the color—a billion little red worms, all swimming in the same direction! These worms were packed together so close that there was barely any water between them, and they wiggled in unison. Because their school was so dense, we could see exactly where it began and where it ended, and we had navigated right into the middle of it.

"Oh, hell," said Whitey, looking over the side of the boat. "Leeches!"

Little Chip drew in a man-sized breath and began to cry on the exhale.

CJ splashed his Cuban heels in the boat's hull. "They suck your blood, don't they?"

"We'll be OK," said Whitey, "just don't panic. They can't get into the boat."

A fearful silence gripped us again. As we advanced, the worms grew thicker and thicker, until they seemed almost substantial enough to walk on. We were disturbing them, churning up millions of worms with our motor. "I didn't see these on my way in," said Whitey, "I hope they don't foul up the propeller." Whitey slowed a bit, which was not reassuring.

Soon we heard a low roar in the distance, which grew in intensity. Frankie was first to recognize the sound. "Oh, shit!" he said. Simultaneously, we sat tall on our benches and looked toward the bay. Not too far away, heading toward us, was the *Miss Atlantic City.* This enormous speedboat, a fifty-footer, sped out of Captain Starns four times a day and took tourists on an ocean thrill-ride. It zoomed so fast that its bow never touched the water but tilted up at a 30° angle, it's hull crashing through the waves so violently that the passengers screamed with each crash and got soaking wet even though they all wore yellow rain coats. And this hulk, capable of speeds of over eighty miles an hour, was bearing down on us at full throttle.

We cowered in our little skiff as the speedboat roared past. It missed us by about twenty feet. But it left in its wake a series of choppy three-foot waves. The laughter and gleeful shouts of the passengers on the *Miss Atlantic City* faded into the distance as we clutched our seats, leaning this way and that to steady the boat as it listed through the waves.

This commotion threw the leeches into tizzy—they were even hopping out of the water. Whitey tried to steer the bow of the boat into the waves, which were big enough so that some of them were breakers, but he failed to bring her around quickly enough. We gripped the rails as she rolled. Wormy waves washed over the sides of the skiff. The worms wiggled on the floor of the boat. When Chip saw the worms in the boat, he stood up and jumped onto a bench, screaming, "Leave me alone!" This made the boat rock out of control. And we capsized. Into the wormy water we went, cooler, sandwiches, sodas, and all. I heard CJ cry, "My shoes!"

Although it was surprisingly simple for us to meet under the boat and grab hold of the benches as Whitey had instructed, when the leeches came to their senses they swarmed around us, and this made us panic. The noise and pandemonium under the boat was deafening. We flailed around trying to shake off the leeches, as the last of the

Miss Atlantic City's waves tried to wrench the boat from our hands. We held onto the benches tightly with one hand and flailed away at the worms with the other. I don't know how Whitey managed to switch the motor off, but he did, and soon the boat was floating in calm water. But I could see the little blood-suckers dangling from the necks and shoulders of my friends, and I could feel them all over me. There was even some blood in the water. "Eww...ewwww...ew," our cries echoed as we peeled off the spiny bloodworms.

Oh my God, I thought, I'll come home looking like a plague victim, covered in bloody bumps, covered in the evidence of my sins! "I'm doomed," I cried.

Chip was wailing like a cat. Whitey put his arms around his little brother and urged him to calm down. "Shhhh, Chip."

"You little snot!" screamed CJ, who was fully clothed. "You sank the boat! You ruined my shoes!"

"Hail Mary, who art in Heaven," said Frankie, pinching desperately at leeches.

"Shut up! Shut up!" demanded Whitey. "Listen!" His words echoed above ours.

We quieted.

"Here's what we have to do. Forget the leeches. We're all going to go out on the same side of the boat. Then we'll grab the rail together. And when I say 'three,' we're gonna push up with all our might and try to right the boat. OK? Just forget the leeches!"

It worked on the third try.

Whitey swam to the other side of the boat to hold her steady, and we clambered aboard. Wet and exhausted, we spent a while, drifting and plucking leeches off our bodies. The bites didn't hurt while we were in the cold water, but now that we were in the boat, each little bite smarted. And we had dozens. But we trembled more with loathing than with pain, because these disgusting creatures were everywhere. They looked like little red earthworms with tough skin. And they seemed to have a mouth on both ends. If you pulled one end off, the other end would try to attach itself to you. Many of the big leeches had little squirmy baby leeches attached to them, sucking their blood. They were so ugly I couldn't bear touching them, but how else could I get them off of me?

CJ had taken off his shirt and found countless worms of different sizes underneath, and that could only mean that the little bites we felt underneath our swim trunks were not figments of our imagination as we hoped. There must be plenty of leeches feasting on the tender flesh of our private parts.

Soon, we were all sitting in the boat stark naked, picking leeches off of every part of us. Another worm appeared just when you thought you had picked them all off. Lucky for us, the part of Atlantic City where we drifted was rarely visited, so there was no one on the nearby jetties or even further away on the boardwalk to see us.

When there were just a few die-hard leeches left to pluck, little Chip stopped crying long enough to mutter, "I think one went up my ass." He was terrified and even paler than usual, his wandering eye vibrating like a guitar string.

"What?"

"There's a leech in my *aaaaaaass!*" he whimpered. And he began to bawl. "Someone take it out!" he pleaded. "Someone take it out!" He bent himself over a bench, showing us his little white butt.

We all looked at Whitey. "He's your brother," said Frankie.

Whitey cautiously approached his brother, peering at his buttocks. Naked as flounders, we watched as Whitey bent down to examine his brother's backside. "Get it out! Get it out!" cried Chip. Whitey was just about to use his fingers to do an exploratory on his brother, when a huge shadow appeared on the water. We looked up. In our panic we hadn't noticed that the *Captain Starns*, a double-decker touring boat that, like the *Miss Atlantic City*, came out of Starns' dock, was approaching. It was bursting with tourists, full to capacity on both tiers, and it was upon us in no time.

Every person on the *Starns* crowded around the rails and gaped at us as they passed. They saw Frankie, CJ, and I sitting naked in the stern of the skiff watching naked Whitey prepare to perform a leechectomy on his brother's naked butt.

Some tourists were laughing. And some looked horrified.

Worst of all, I thought I saw Izzy Goldfarb's grandchildren, the girl and two boys, on that ship. Dressed identically, in tennis sweaters and white shorts, they gazed down at us from behind the top rail of the *Captain Starns* and laughed, as we sat in our craft, mortified, trying to twist ourselves into as modest a contortion as we could. They'd surely report what they'd seen.

"Was that the Goldfarb kids up there?" I asked.

Whitey looked up. "No! Where?"

The laughter faded as the ship moved off. Frankie, who was not one to take humiliation sitting down, got to his feet, angered. Facing the *Starns,* he bid the ship *bon voyage* by putting one hand on his hip and pointing to his penis with the other. He swiveled his hips as he pointed to himself and said, "Whyn't ya take a picture, assholes. It lasts longer!" And they probably did.

This time, at least, the waves from this ship didn't topple us. Whitey gave his brother's backside a big-brotherly swat and assured him that there were no worms in his butt, although Chip kept crying and said he could feel worms crawling in his belly.

In the distance, Wasserman's cooler floated off toward England. Carefully, so as not to rock the boat, we put our trunks back on, one at a time. Suddenly struck by the humor of the whole thing, CJ burst out laughing.

"Gosh, Frankie, what are you going to tell Mr. Wasserman?" I asked.

Wringing out his shirt over the water, CJ roared.

We did not find that beach we had set out to rediscover, the ocean's nursery. We didn't try. After our run-in with the red tide, all we wanted to do was lose the skiff. When we were dressed and calm, and Whitey had somehow got the motor started, we sped off at full speed toward the bay. We didn't want to run into the *Miss Atlantic City* on her return voyage.

We reached the dock where Whitey's father kept the boat and moored it, but we didn't go right home. The marina behind Starns was too inviting a pool to pass up. The smooth waters by the dock offered a salve to our wounds. We were charmed by the sound of the boats bobbing at their moorings, the creaking of the docks, and the shrieking of the gulls. The docks provided good diving platforms. And the water there was a little warmer than in the ocean. So we stayed and swam in this natural pool until we were happy again. But not CJ. He spent the time sitting on the dock in his briefs, letting his clothes dry on the dock and grieving for his ruined shoes; and not Chip, who curled on the dock in a fetal position, whining and repeating that he had a leech in his guts.

As the afternoon sun slanted warm and weak from the city side, we walked home on the boardwalk. Whitey had to carry Chip for a few blocks.

THE FIRST thing my mother noticed after I slammed the kitchen door to announce my entrance were the suspicious marks on my neck. Before I could sit down, she grabbed my arm and moved me into the light of the screen door to examine the mysterious red marks on my neck. She pulled my T-shirt over my head and tossed it aside, exposing my torso riddled with bites. "Oy!" she exclaimed. "What have you done to yourself this time?" She had been busy cooking so she had her trusty spatula in her hand, and she pointed it at me. "Do you have impetigo again? Have you been climbing between the rocks? If you don't stop hanging around with those bums, you're going to wind up dead." I had half a mind to agree with her, but she was too angry to encourage. She sounded as if she had been storing it up all day.

"They're just mosquito bites," I explained. "There were a million mosquitoes at Starns, and they attacked us in swarms."

Harry, seated at his usual spot at the table, chimed in, "They don't look like mosquito bites."

Mom waited for an explanation, withdrawing slightly to get a better view of my condition. She folded her arms, waiting for a truer account.

"They're mosquito bites," I insisted. "It's just that I've been scratching them." The sores did look something like scratched mosquito bites.

"Listen to me, buddy-boy," Mom snapped. "Those hoodlums you hang around with are bad eggs!" She pointed her spatula out the window where the hoodlums roamed. "And it's got to stop, d'you hear?" She looked me in the eye. "I've been worrying about you all day! And now look at you!"

"Worrying all day, worrying all day." Harry stoked the fire.

Mom lowered the boom. "I've had it," she said. "I'm done. I don't want you hanging around with Frankie or any of those boys any more! Same thing every summer! Broken toes, impetigo, calls from the beach patrol.... That's it! I've had it!" She turned to check on the hamburgers in the electric broiler. They had a few minutes to cook. She turned back to me, looking irate, trying to diagnose my sores.

"But—but—" I decided not to push it until Mom cooled.

For good measure, Harry said, "They're not mosquito bites," and he swung out of his seat to get a closer look.

There was a tense moment during which Harry and Mom walked around me scanning my torso, waiting for plausible explanation.

But I said nothing. What could I say? That my friends and I took an unauthorized ride in a boat that was far too small to hold us, with no life jackets, and we tipped the thing over into a swarm of leeches? I don't think so. "Those mosquitos were murder," I said.

Mom's anger subsided a little as she finished cooking and removed the hamburgers. She was probably afraid to pursue the truth. She said, "Come with me." She put down her spatula, and led me into the bathroom. There she took a bottle of calamine lotion and some cotton balls from the medicine chest and daubed each bite. This felt good. "Ew," she said, "these look more like spider bites or something...."

I felt the urge to scratch my belly, but Mom said, "Don't *mitch-uh*!" and slapped my hand away. "You'll *mitch-uh* it on good, and then there'll be trouble."

"Mom," I said, "I've been Frankie's friend for a lot of summers. And I've known Big Ned for almost as long. I can't just ignore them. They live on the street. It wouldn't be...right." I felt Mom softening as she ran out of sores to pat. "Honest, Mom, all we did today was walk to Captain Starns, check out the porpoises, and walk back. Then we took a swim, and I came home. I couldn't help getting these bites."

My hand went automatically to scratch my shoulder.

"Stop! Don't *mitch*-uh! You told me this morning that you would swim with *us* on Vermont Avenue beach, didn't you?"

"Yeah, but—"

"'But me no 'but's,'" Mom objected, "and listen." She stopped dabbing and sat on the edge of the bathtub. "I will allow you to hang around with Frankie and the others for a few hours in the evening after dinner to play ball or whatever. But, for the next two weeks you are going to swim at Vermont Avenue beach with your brother and me, so I can keep an eye on you. I don't know what you've been up to, but I know it's not good. Harry hints at things I don't like, and I can't take the worry. If your buddies want to swim with you, they can swim at our beach."

I negotiated, "Can I hang with my friends in the morning, before we go on the beach?"

"No!" said mom. She stood up and shooed me into the kitchen where dinner needed her attention. I took my place at the table.

This punishment was going to swipe a serious chunk of fun out of my vacation.

Meanwhile, Fred had returned from work. "Hate, hate, hate!" he muttered. His tone, more serious than usual, demanded attention.

Mom took the bait. "What's the matter, Fred?"

"That slave-driver Moishe made me clean up after this lady that puked all over the floor of the store this afternoon," said Fred. "And all he had to clean it with was tissues!"

"Eewwww, *phoy*," exclaimed Harry.

"Probably drunk," said Mom.

I said, "She mighta seen the fake vomit you guys sell and...."

Fred looked at the ceiling and clenched his fists at his sides. "HATE! HATE! HATE!"

Mom set out crunchy string beans, and two huge sliced tomatoes. She must have gotten back from the beach in time to catch the truck with the guy who sang, *"Jersey tomatoes, three pounds a quarter, here!"*

During dinner, Fred looked at my calamine dotted body and said, "Whatcha got there, Rich? Looks like ya got bit by some bloodworms." Harry and Mom looked at me.

"Mosquito bites," I said.

"Right," said Fred. He returned to eating his hamburger and anticipating his rendezvous later that evening with the leviathan that swam through his imagination.

3.
La Belle Dame Sans Merci

A few pages after "The Song of the Wandering Aengus," I find the ballad "La Belle Dame Sans Merci" by John Keats.

I saw two belle filles *walking along the water's edge a while ago. One* belle fille, *slim and boyish, wore a white bikini that hardly covered her. The wind blew a riot of colorless hair behind her. The other fille was dark, and curvier. Her bright yellow suit contrasted with her complexion. They were walking fast, exercising, and it made me think of "The Love Song of J. Alfred Prufrock." I thought of the line, "I have heard the mermaids singing each to each..." and I wondered if* Twice-Read Poems *had "Prufrock." So I looked in the index; it didn't. They were pretty girls. I'm glad I've reached an age where such a sight does not muddle the rest of my day with futile fantasies.*

Like "Aengus," "La Belle Dame" fits into the genre of fantasy— which is a positive—even if there are no monsters or laser guns. Just an old-fashioned knight, who has been brought low by the daughter of a fairy after they spend an idyllic afternoon together. They meet by chance in the woods. She hops onto the knight's saddle. They sing songs, weave garlands, and go back to her place. There she feeds him manna dew. And then he "shut(s) her wild eyes with kisses four." That's good, that's sex; sex is a positive. After sex, the fairy's child, an expert herbalist, casts the knight into a trance-like sleep, where he dreams of a parade of pale warriors—knights, kings, and princes—who warn him that he is, like them, a victim of La Belle Dame Sans Merci, who makes men fall in love with her and then disappears. Finally, as foretold in the dream, the knight awakes alone, abandoned by La Belle Dame. And now, paralyzed by grief, he lies on the wet ground, somewhere in the woods, distraught and unable to go home, even though the weather is getting nasty.

Who can't relate to a simple story of love's heartache? Who has not been disappointed by love? This poem will be in the curriculum for sure, right after Aengus, *as a counterbalance to* Aengus's *opitmism.*

From where I'm sitting on Montgomery Avenue Beach, if I were to look to my left, I would see, just a mile down the boardwalk, the place where the Deauville Hotel once stood, and that's where I worked when I suffered my first heartbreak, at the hands of une belle dame.

I had just finished my first year of college. I still spent summers with Mom and Harry on Vermont Avenue, though the neighborhood was deteriorating. Mom was trying to sell the house. Dad had died. Fred was married. My oldest brother had expatriated to New Zealand. All my old friends from Vermont Avenue were gone. I heard from one of my workmates at the Deauville who knew Frankie Talone from high school, that he had enlisted in the army and gone to Vietnam. Rita had moved to Las Vegas. And Frankie's sister Pat, whom I never saw except as a shadow behind a window screen, had joined a Hare Krishna sect in New York.

I was working as a line runner in the hotel's dining room. A few blocks down the boardwalk on South Carolina Avenue, there was a clammy little dive bar called the Bluebird Café, where the afternoon bartender was a petite blonde named Ro. My coworkers and I went to "The Bird" after work because a draft beer in a frosty mug cost fifty cents, and they didn't bother checking IDs. Ro was usually behind the bar when we arrived.

I fell hard for Ro. She was cute and cheerful, always smiling and energetic, and she knew how a seashore barmaid should dress. Her uniform consisted of cutoffs that were completely cut off, a bikini top, and flip-flops; in other words, less was more, and this uniform was custom-made for her small shape. Her tip jar overflowed.

Everyone flirted with Ro, so it was an easy thing to do. I surprised myself one evening when, at the end of Ro's shift, I summoned the courage to ask her if I could walk her home, and she doubled my surprise when she agreed. She took me to bed that night, and my inexperience was laughable. I'd never been in bed with a naked woman. In my eagerness I groped her body like a drowning man. Just as she was chuckling and pushing me away, saying, "Settle down, Rich. Not yet," I tried to mount her and, in my state of high excitement, I came, prematurely, on her thigh. I was mortified. But Ro was unconcerned. She found my clumsiness either refreshing or challenging. Adeptly, she took matters into her own hands. After admonishing me as though I were a naughty puppy, she gave me some useful instructions, and allowed me a couple more tries. I soon got the hang of it. When she sent me home that night, I was infatuated. When she took me home the next night, I was done for.

After that, I ached with impatience all day at work, dying to run down to the Bird where another chance with Ro might await—and it happened a few more times.

I assumed she felt the same way toward me as I felt toward her—smitten. Which was not the case. Most likely, she was simply amusing herself with my deflowering, and she saw my feverish persistence as an expression of gratitude. I don't know; I was in an altered state. I ignored the fact that she left the bar at the end of her shift with many of the customers who crowded into the Bluebird Café at beer o'clock. She was especially fond of lifeguards, and she sometimes left with two or three of them. There was a mustachioed policeman whose attentions she enjoyed. And one time I saw her leave with the old caricature artist who worked on the boardwalk nearby. He was at least seventy years old and usually too drunk to complete a sentence. She had to help him out the door. But my state of denial was such that I believed that when Ro left the bar with someone else, she was going dancing with friends, or getting a ride home, or something equally innocent. I never entertained the idea that she was conducting an extensive sexual experiment, and I was one of many guinea pigs.

One fateful afternoon, sick of my moony behavior around Ro, and the obscenely generous tips I left, my workmate at the Deauville, Sam, disabused me of my romantic infatuation. "Looka here, bro," he said. "I can't let you keep makin' a fool a'yourself. That chick, Ro, man. She be makin' it with every guy in the bar. You understand what I'm sayin'? Including me. If you want to keep bonin' her that's one thing, but you gotta git dat love shit outa yo' haid, man, d'ya hear?"

I was momentarily stunned. Then everything became clear. I looked at Ro. She was having a laugh with her policeman, who stood with his elbows on the bar in full flirtation mode. I noted the drunken caricature artist swaying on his stool and shuddered. I didn't argue with Sam. He was trying to help me—as he did in the kitchens of the Deauville; and besides, Sam was tall and muscular with zero body fat; he played football for Rutgers. Not someone you'd want to argue with. I just left the bar, mid-beer, without tipping.

As I walked home on the deserted boardwalk, somewhere around New Jersey Avenue I saw a big dog on the beach sitting up and looking straight at me. His eyes followed me, and he had a big smile on his face. Then the dog laughed! This crazy dog was laughing at me! So I stopped. He barked a couple of times and laughed even harder. Catching the dog's eye, I thought I understood the joke, and I laughed along with him. We howled a little too. So there I was, all alone on the boardwalk, with night descending, laughing and howling with a crazy dog. If he were a poet-dog, I guess he would have said, "Oh, what can ail thee, knight-at-arms...."

I didn't go back to the Bluebird that summer. The thought of Ro in the arms of those other guys—especially the caricature artist—made me wince. She was as soft as a rose petal, and when she made love her eyes rolled back into her head like she was having a seizure. She moaned from a deeper part of her being than her size would seem to allow. For her, sex was a transcendental experience. She didn't belong with a stinking old caricature artist.

To this day I cringe with embarrassment when I think about our first night together.

●

AFTER dinner, I exercised my right to meet my friends in the evening. I found Frankie and Whitey sitting on the curb in front of Whitey's apartment talking in low tones. Like me, they were covered in "mosquito bites," and like me, their bites had been dabbed with calamine. Up the street, Big Ned was hurling a sponge ball at a strike zone painted on a brick wall. Each strike echoed with a loud *fwap*.

Whitey and Frankie stopped talking when I approached. I pointed at Ned. "Doesn't he ever let up?"

"Naw," said Frankie. "He's pitched five perfect games in a row and hit something like thirteen home runs this season."

Ned grunted, then *fwap*.

"He looks like he's twenty years old," I said. "Is it fair for him to play in the Little League?"

"He eats his Wheaties," said Frankie.

"So what were you guys talking about when I walked up?" I asked.

"Baseball," said Whitey.

Frankie looked at Whitey, who reddened. "Should I tell him?" asked Frankie.

Whitey shook his head.

Frankie changed the subject, "What did your mother say when she saw your bites?"

"I told her they were mosquito bites. But I got in trouble anyway."

"Me and Frankie told his Aunt Rita everything," Whitey said. "She thought it was hilarious."

Frankie laughed. "Yeah, especially the part about Chip thinking a leech crawled up his ass. She's probably still laughing—"

"It's not funny," said Whitey, shoving Frank's shoulder. "Chip's shook up. I put him to bed. He was crying and sucking his thumb like a baby until he got to sleep."

"I never see your Dad anymore," I said.

"He works most nights in the summer."

"And days," said Frank

"Well," I said, "my mom was mad at *you* guys because I was full of sores. And she said that I can't swim with you for two weeks. I have to sit on Vermont beach with her and Harry."

Whitey was too preoccupied to respond, but Frankie sympathized. "That ought to be fun," he said.

"I'll die."

"Breaks," said Frank.

Then there was silence, except for the *fwap* of Ned's ball against the wall.

"C'mon, what were you talking about before I got here?" They looked at each other. "Were you talking about me? What did I do?"

"You didn't do nothing," Frankie assured me. "Whitey was just getting something off his chest, something I can't repeat." Whitey slumped.

"What? *What?*"

Frankie started to spill the beans, "Whitey was just telling me that—" but before he could finish, Whitey reached over and covered Frankie's mouth with his hand. Frankie pulled loose, and he stopped talking for a moment so Whitey would settle. Then he finished his sentence: "—he's in *loooove*." Frankie punctuated the word *love* with a few air kisses. Whitey's eyes widened. He jumped off the curb, and pulled Frankie up by the arm. "You bastard!" Whitey said, twisting Frankie's arm. Frankie laughed. I stood back, because Whitey looked genuinely angry. He swung Frankie to the ground and stood over him pulling on his arm. But Frankie didn't fight back. He just made like Whitey was hurting him badly so Whitey would let go. Ned, up the street, stopped pitching and turned to see what was going on.

Frankie held his shoulder, as though he were in pain. "What's the matter, lover-boy? All I said was what you told me." Whitey threw Frankie's arm aside, and then turned and walked back to the curb. He sat and looked across the street.

Still lying in the street, Frankie said, "He's far gone, far gone."

I helped Frankie up, and we went over and sat on either side of Whitey.

"Do you want to know who stole his heart?" Frankie asked, putting his hand on Whitey's shoulder. Whitey squirmed away. Frankie nodded across the street.

I had not noticed but, across the street, on the porch of Goldfarb's Guest House, Izzy's granddaughter sat rocking gently in a wicker chair. She had been watching us the whole time. Newly showered and deeply tanned, she sat surrounded by the many potted geraniums that Mrs. Goldfarb kept on the guesthouse porch. Her hair, held down in front by a barrette, broke loose around her head, an aura of kinky waves.

"Goldfarb's granddaughter?" I asked.

"Yep," said Frankie, "I'm afraid so. Goldfarb's goddamn skinny granddaughter."

"Her name is Ellen," said Whitey, looking down now between his knees at the gutter. Ellen gazed calmly back, the way girls look at boys when boys act in ways they find peculiar. She rocked a few more rocks in her chair; then she rose and vanished into the house.

Whitey said, "I have to look in on Chip," and he stood up to go. "You guys have to keep your mouths shut about this, see?" And he was gone.

Frankie brought me up to date. "He's been sneaking out at night and talking to her."

"You mean she knows he likes her?"

"Yup," said Frank.

"And she likes him?"

"Yup."

"How? I mean, where do they meet?" I asked.

"He talks to her in her bedroom," said Frankie.

"Her bedroom! He gets into her bedroom?"

"No, stupid. He knows where her bedroom window is, and he talks to her through her window. Do you see that wood fence there in the alley next to the house?" Frankie pointed across the street.

"Yeah."

"Well, Whitey climbs onto that fence, and he stands up on it, so he can see into her bedroom."

"Whoa," I whispered.

"He says he talks to her until he's too tired to keep his balance on the fence. She never wants him to leave—according to him."

"You're kidding. She must really like him." I felt a pang of jealousy. I never dreamed Izzy's granddaughter was approachable. "Can't he just go to the door and ask if he can see her?"

"No way," said Frankie, "She's not allowed."

"How does he know if he hasn't tried?"

"She told him. She said her grandfather promised her parents she wouldn't mingle with the neighborhood kids while she was visiting. She's from Cherry Hill." Frankie said *Cherry Hill* with something like an English accent.

"Gee, that's tough."

"Whitey's nuts," said Frankie. "She's not even good lookin'."

"Oh yes she is!" I said. The words bounced right out, and Frankie looked at me like I had a screw loose.

Then a familiar twinkle lit up Frank's eyes. "I'll tell you what," he said. "Let's get lost for about an hour, until it's dark. Then we'll come back and see if lover-boy pays his girlie a visit tonight. We can keep a lookout from over there in Whitey's alley. We'll watch the whole show. I got a new set of binoculars I want to try out."

"OK."

Frankie scooted up the steps of his apartment to get his binoculars, which turned out to be those toy pop-open opera-glasses with the inscription WELCOME TO ATLANTIC CITY on them. We went up the street and sat on the rail of the boardwalk where we could watch Ned practice and wait until dark. I spent the time looking out to sea with the binoculars, and Frankie watched Ned.

Ned was working hard, sweating through his T-shirt. Each pitch dipped and rose and then exploded against the bricks. *Fwap!* As the sun set, Frankie heckled Ned, timing his taunts for maximum effect. "Miss! MISS! Gimme a kiss! Whyn't ya try underhanded—go faster? Watch the car!" But Ned just grunted and fired, oblivious to Frank's jeers. *Fwap*, another strike. "Good girl!" said Frank.

When it was dark, we left. Ned continued firing his sponge ball, alone in a circle of light cast by a street lamp. I suppose he heard applause for each strike from some imaginary fans that crowded in the darkness at the edge of the circle of light. *Fwap.*

Instead of walking down Vermont Avenue, right to Whitey's driveway, Frankie decided we should go down Victoria Avenue, the next street over. That way, Whitey would be sure not to see us. At the house on Victoria directly behind Whitey's, we could hop a fence and sneak into Whitey's backyard. We could then slip undetected into the darkness of Whitey's driveway, the perfect place to eavesdrop on the lovers across the street. No one would suspect a thing. And all that sneaking around would be cool.

Everything went as planned. But as we snuck down Whitey's drive, I heard a pathetic whimpering coming from inside Whitey's apartment. It gave me the creeps. I couldn't see into the apartment—it was dark—but I knew it was Chip, who couldn't sleep and lay sobbing in his bed.

I stopped at Chip's window. "Hey, Frankie," I whispered, "shouldn't we do something about Chip? He's crying."

Frankie was already in position. "Are you kidding?" Giggling with excitement, he waved me over. "Check it out!"

I joined him. He pointed across the street to Goldfarb's Guest House. Mrs. Goldfarb, Ellen's grandmother, and some other ladies were sitting on the flowery porch chatting away, completely oblivious to the fact that Whitey was standing on a wooden fence that ran along the side of the house, and he was speaking earnestly toward a window just above his head—Ellen's bedroom window. We could see her shadow on the window screen. Whitey stood on the fence as easily as you please and whispered in a voice so low it was concealed by the chirp of crickets and some soft music that came from Ellen's radio.

When you're young and so in love as we
And bewildered by the world we see....

Now we knew every driveway, alley, and fence in the neighborhood, and we knew that the fence that Whitey was standing on was pretty narrow and shaky. Yet Whitey stood upright and balanced himself without so much as a wobble, as though he were being held aloft by magnetism. He even managed to throw in some hand gestures as he spoke, and still he didn't falter. Ellen leaned on her windowsill and gazed down at Whitey. She'd lost her barrette, and the shadow of her wavy hair filled the window.

Meanwhile, Frankie and I nearly busted a gut to keep from laughing out loud and blowing our cover. What amused Frankie and me so much was how unaware Mrs. Goldfarb and her friends were of what was taking place on the other side of the house. I mean, there they were, Mrs. Goldfarb and her klatch of biddies, jabbering away a mile a minute in Yiddish—probably about how today's parents don't watch their kids closely enough—and right under their noses, not twenty feet away, Whitey was standing on their fence, seducing Ellen.

The scene proved too much for Frankie. Looking through his binoculars, he began to giggle and couldn't stop. "Look at the puss on old Mrs. Goldfarb," said Frankie. "She looks like a bulldog." He handed me the binoculars and clamped both hands over his mouth, trying to restrain his laughter. I took a peek through the glasses. And, yes, the old lady did have a bit of bulldog about her. But it was how heedless they were to the scene on the side of the house that was so funny. Like Frankie, I started to chuckle. And that made Frank laugh a little louder, and that made me laugh a little louder, until we were both flat-out laughing our asses off. Instinctively, Whitey looked in our direction. He knew it was us hiding in the shadows of his driveway. But our laughter broke the spell that kept him aloft. He wavered, teetering on one foot as his arms flailed. And then he toppled over and fell noisily into the next door neighbor's begonia patch.

Ellen quickly withdrew from her window.

All this hullabalooloo made the old folks on Goldfarb's porch stir. They suspected mischief. Mrs. Goldfarb waddled down the steps to investigate what was happening in her breezeway, but Whitey was long gone. And we disappeared into Whitey's backyard just as swiftly. Mrs. Goldfarb returned to her friends, saying something about cats.

Moments later, Whitey joined us behind his apartment. He had run down New Hampshire Avenue to Oriental and come up Victoria, as we had, so as not to be seen. He bounced easily over his back fence and into his yard. We thought he'd want to kill us, but he was too excited to be angry. "She's great," he said breathlessly. "She's just great!" Whitey looked into the heavens. "Thank you," he said.

"Oh, brother," said Frankie. "You know, Whitey, if you keep this up, you're gonna get caught."

"Well, what else can I do?" asked Whitey.

"Can't you arrange to meet her someplace, like down by the jetty or something?" asked Frank.

"Not a chance," insisted Whitey. "She's not allowed out at night."

"But you can't even touch her," said Frank.

"How about on the beach during the day," I suggested. "You could both take a walk at the same time and meet."

"She sits on a beach way up in Margate somewhere," said Whitey.

"Oh, *Maw-gate*," I said, mimicking Frank's English accent.

"It's like this," said Whitey. "Ellen is visiting her grandparents, and her mom and dad aren't here. They're back in Cherry Hill. So the Goldfarbs watch over her like hawks. She can't breathe without their permission."

We paused. The crickets were raising a ruckus in the yard, and we could hear little Chip in bed, moaning like he had a bad cramp. Whitey looked baffled. He suddenly squatted and uttered a disgusted "Harumph!"

"Hmmm," said Frankie. "We need a plan."

"Let's go in," said Whitey, "I have to help Chip."

We entered Whitey's living room. "Wipe your feet," he said.

The room was tidy. There was a sofa and a chair in the same plaid pattern. A clock in the shape of a ship's steering wheel hung on one wall, and a round convex mirror hung on another. Under the mirror was a wooden cabinet which I assumed concealed the TV. On the floor lay a carpet that looked like woven rope. There were no knickknacks. Incredibly, the place had no damp basement smell; instead it smelled like the carpet, like jute.

Frankie and I sat on the couch while Whitey went to console Chip. We could hear him soothing his little brother in soft tones. Chip was still harping on the leeches. His complaints were so severe they made me wonder for a moment if there might be a leech somewhere inside me, but I shook it off.

"CJ was right," said Frankie. "That little kid *is* a snot. I wish he'd shut it."

"Aw, Frankie, leave him alone," I said. "You act like those leeches didn't even bother you."

"They didn't."

"Well, they gave me the willies, and Chip's just a kid."

"I wasn't afraid for a minute," said Frankie.

"You were praying."

"I was not."

"Were too."

"Was not."

Whitey emerged. "Shhh, I think Chip might go to sleep. If he tells my dad about that boat ride, I'm screwed." He fell onto a chair.

"Know what, Whitey?" Frankie leaned back on the couch with the look of a man with a plan. Something was brewing. "I think I know a way where you could meet Ellen secretly."

"How? I can't go to her house. And she can't come out unless she's with her brothers. She says her parents think us kids who live here all year 'round are a lot of tramps. That's the word she used, 'tramps.' She's not even allowed to talk to us. Old man Goldfarb calls my dad 'the Nazi across the street!' It's impossible. I'll just have to keep using the fence."

"Wait a minute," Frankie began. "Listen. Richie doesn't live here all year 'round, does he?

"No."

"And he's rich, right?"

"Rich? Me?"

"And Richie's Jewish," Frankie continued. "Just like them, right? Old Goldfarb and Richie's parents are friends. See what I'm saying?"

Whitey's eyes widened.

"What *are* you saying?" I asked.

Frankie pointed at me then Whitey. "*You* can deliver Ellen to Whitey."

"Huh? But...noooo—"

"Look, here's what we're going to do," said Frankie, turning toward Whitey. "Tomorrow night when you talk to Ellen, tell her that Richie is going to stop by for her on the day after tomorrow. What's that, Wednesday? That'll give us time to perfect the plan. Ellen will tell her grandparents that she has a date with Richie. Wednesday, after dinner, Richie will stop up at Goldfarb Manor and ask the 'Farbs if Ellen can come out and take a walk on the boards. The 'Farbs are sure to OK that, and Richie will deliver Ellen to you on the boardwalk at New Hampshire Avenue. Simple."

"I'm not rich," I said, "I'm—"

"Why wait two days? I'll go back and tell her tonight," said Whitey. "We'll do it tomorrow."

"No," said Frank. "Too soon. There might be something we haven't thought of. Keep your pants on—"

"Wait a minute. You're saying I'm going to pretend I'm taking Ellen out on a date?"

"Yep," said Frankie, "and don't complain. You owe it to Whitey for taking you out on his dad's boat."

"Where I almost died," I said. The idea of knocking on the Goldfarbs' door, looking old Izzy in the eye, and tricking him troubled me. Besides, taking Ellen out on a date was something I wouldn't have the courage to do on my own behalf, so where was I going to find the courage to do it for Whitey? "I don't like this," I said. "I've known Mr. Goldfarb all my life. I can't lie to him like that...."

"Shame on you!" said Frankie.

"Shame on— Why?"

"Here me and Whitey have been your friends for—what is it, like five years? Every summer. And we *wait* for you to come down in the summer, because we like you. And we show you all the swimming holes and fun places to go that no one else knows about, and you won't even do Whitey a little favor like this. Do you think other kids who come down for the summer know the stuff you know because of us? Shame—on—you!"

"Three years," I said.

"What?"

"I've known you for three years."

Together, Whitey and Frankie looked at me expectantly. If it had just been Frankie, I'd have probably told him to buzz off, since he'd gotten me into so many jams over the years. I didn't owe him squat. But Whitey was a good guy and deserved a favor. He'd risked a lot to give us that boat ride, and it wasn't his fault we were covered in bumps and calamine lotion. Actually, all things considered, I'd had a pretty nice day in Whitey's boat. Izzy, I reasoned, was making a big mistake about Whitey. He wasn't a tramp or a Nazi. Not at all. He was generous and good natured. He took care of Chip, and he was probably the one who kept his apartment so neat. If it weren't for Whitey back at Brigantine, Frankie would probably have killed a whole generation of sea creatures.

"C'mon," said Whitey, "I'll owe you."

"Well," I said, "OK, but I'm not going to like it."

Frankie and Whitey leaned back and smiled. Frankie's smile was mischievous. Whitey's was hopeful. "All right. This is good," said Frank. "We'll work out the details."

"I'm not rich," I said. "Art Fanelli over on New Hampshire is rich. His dad's trucks are all over town."

But Frankie and Whitey had recommenced a game of made-ya-flinch that they must have started before I came on the scene, and they paid me no mind.

I COULDN'T get to sleep that night. Not because I had a problem with lying; lying, in general, was fine. You had to lie in order to have fun. But lying to Izzy Goldfarb bothered me. I didn't know him well enough to lie to him and then expect to be forgiven if I got caught. Lying to my parents was one thing. I had an account with them. There was stuff I'd done on the positive side to cancel the stuff on the negative side. And besides, they were my parents, so they were obliged to forgive me. But Izzy? I had no account with him. He would only have this one offense to know me by, and he had no obligation to forgive me. If he found me out, he'd hate me forever.

He might hold it against my parents. And they needed Izzy. Not only did he fix the stuff that broke in our apartment, but he watched our place during the winter. He and my father were buddies. They liked to babble together in Yiddish. Betraying Izzy could be a disaster.

And the possibility of getting caught in this lie was greater than usual. Usually, I lied about a single event, like going to Brigantine or swimming in a forbidden spot. Those lies were controllable. We would take a trip, tell a lie, and it was over. But bearding for Whitey might require many lies—perhaps a lie a night, for many nights. Who could tell how many dates Whitey and Ellen would go on? Very risky. And who was the beneficiary of these lies? Who was going to have all the fun? Not me.

I resolved to change my mind and tell Frankie and Whitey that I couldn't be a stand-in.

But then, I thought about how I needed my seashore friends. Without them I'd be stuck sitting on the beach all summer with my mother and brother. No more adventures. Besides, when you came right down to it, it was Ellen, not me, who was telling the big lie. I was just a middleman, a cog, a small potato. And she probably didn't have a lot to worry about because she was Izzy's granddaughter, and she had an even better account with Izzy than I had with my parents—she had a *grandfather* account, the best kind. He would forgive her in no time. And I did want to do Whitey a favor. And I surely wanted to meet Ellen. She was pretty and classy. If it were not for this situation, I'd never get to know her. So this was a good opportunity to meet an attractive girl. I liked her.

All this thinking was keeping me awake. I calmed myself by fantasizing what it would be like to stop up for Ellen and take her out myself.

I have to admit, in spite of myself, it was soothing to sit on the beach with Harry and Mom during the next two days, so long as I didn't think of my impending "date." The weather was hot, and I spent a lot of time swimming alone, which is not a bad way to swim. When I came out of the ocean, my mom gave me plums and peaches from her beach bag and cool water from her Thermos. Late in the afternoon, I dozed in the sun and baked as the sound of waves breaking and kids laughing filled my dreamy boredom.

Harry spent his days poring over the *Inquirer* and making calculations from the Phillies' box scores. He worked in a spiral notebook, mumbling to himself and doing a lot of arithmetic, until he had fashioned some neat little charts. I envied Harry's ability to amuse himself.

In the evening, Frankie discussed further details for his plan while we did our usual stuff—stickball, pinball, cycling. The second evening we decided to see how far up the island we could ride our bikes if we only used small streets and parking lots, no main streets or the boardwalk. We got all the way to Tennessee Avenue. Art Fanelli joined me and Frank. He had a new Raleigh bike, a three-speed. He let me try it. I had never ridden an English racer, and it made me reevaluate my bulky Schwinn.

Frankie's new wrinkle in the plan was that I'd have to hide during Whitey's date so no one would see me—maybe go way up the boardwalk. But I figured the only people I needed to hide from were the Goldfarbs, and they never went out at night. Who else would care?

He also told me exactly where I should hand Ellen over to Whitey, and that I should meet Ellen at that same place at ten o'clock to take her home. No doubt Whitey spent these evenings perched on his fence, refining plans with Ellen.

By the the time the evening of my assignment rolled around, I'd accepted my part in the play, and I dressed myself as though I were going on a date. After showering before dinner, I applied a drop of Vitalis to my hair and carefully constructed a neat part and a pompadour. Instead of my usual cutoffs and T-shirt, I dressed in Bermuda shorts and a polo shirt. I even considered using a dash of my brother's Old Spice, but I didn't want to arouse suspicion. I tried to convince myself that stopping up for Ellen would be simple—just a quick hello and out the door—but it didn't ease my jitters.

As I dressed I could hear Fred at the dinner table telling Mom and Harry about the latest atrocity committed by his boss. At work that day Fred had been ordered to cut a hundred cardboard boxes into a thousand little cardboard squares that his boss wanted to use as price markers. Fred was fuming. "The only scissors they had were the kind you use in elementary school. The kind with round edges! The ones that kill your fingers! Look at my fingers!" Fred drew to his usual climax. "Hate, HATE, *HATE*!"

I entered the kitchen quietly and took my place at the table. Mom put a plate heaped with spaghetti and meatballs before me. My favorite.

"Whoa," said Harry, noticing how spiffed up I was, "where are you going tonight?"

"On the boards," I answered shortly, "with Frankie and Whitey."

"Who is this Whitey guy?" my mother asked as she set a container of Parmesan cheese on the table. "Do I know him?"

"He's lived here for years," I said. "He's the guy with the white crewcut. Nice kid."

"I'll bet," said Mom.

"He is. He's the responsible type. Takes care of his little brother and does things around the house. You'd like him. Definitely not a bum."

"Uh huh," said Mom.

Harry was perplexed. He prided himself on always knowing what I was up to, but I could tell he didn't have a clue as to what my combed hair and polo shirt meant.

"Well," said Fred, calm now as he speared a meatball with his fork, "I'll be fishing in the surf off States Avenue tonight." He looked my way, "And I'm feeling lucky. If you see me from the boards, stop on down. Who knows, I might need someone to carry my gear while I haul home a big fish."

Halfway through dinner, Frankie and Whitey stopped up for me. They looked in through the screen door. Mom, addressing Frankie with the usual irony, said, "Is that you, Frankie Talone? You come in here, you bum."

Frank and Whitey came sheepishly through the door. "Good evening, Mrs. Sugarman," said Frankie, smiling with his own brand of irony. Whitey tried to make himself invisible.

"Don't 'good evening' me, you bad egg," Mom teased. "Why did Richie come home covered with mosquito bites the other day? Huh? Speak up."

"Well, Mrs. Sugarman, we all got a lot of mosquito bites the other day," said Frankie. He could suck up better than Eddie Haskell if he needed to. Whitey, who was hiding behind Frankie, nodded. As proof of his sincerity, Frankie raised his shirt for a moment to show the bites on his belly.

Fred looked over to me and cocked one eyebrow as if to say, "What did you guys get yourselves into?" But nobody noticed.

"Golly, Mrs. Sugarman, that spaghetti looks good," said Frank, deftly changing the subject.

"You're too late, Mr. Talone," said Mom, and she tilted the pot toward Frankie to show it was empty. "Let Richie eat his dinner, now. You boys can wait for him out front." She pointed out the door with the ladle she held on spaghetti night, and they left, pushing each other like vaudevillians.

"OK, Mrs. Sugarman," said Frankie on the way out. "Rita loved the pattern you gave her for the baby sweater." Mom had given Rita that pattern two summers ago.

Whitey mumbled something that sounded like, "Nice to see you ma'am."

When my friends were out of earshot, Harry said, "Richie's up to something. He and Whitey are dressed up, and Frankie's not."

"Oh please!" I objected. "Are you Sherlock Holmes or something?"

"Eat your dinner," said Mom, before a controversy could begin. "I want to get cleaned up before *Jack Benny* comes on. Want to watch with me, Harry?"

"There's a night game on the radio," said Harry. And this was good, because I could go about my business and not worry about Harry or Mom sitting outside and noticing my comings and goings.

After dinner, as I walked down the driveway to the front of my house, Frankie ambushed me. He grabbed my arm and rushed me toward the street as though his plan were running behind schedule. "It's all set," he said. "Ellen told her grandparents that she's going out with you, and they consented."

"How do you know?" I asked.

"Ellen told Whitey," said Frankie. "Let's go."

When we reached the street, we met an eager Whitey, and Frankie called a huddle to design the next play. "Whitey," he said, "now's the time. You head out for the boardwalk up on New Hampshire. Me and Richie will stay here and count to a hundred. That'll give you plenty of time to get into position. Then Richie will stop by for Ellen. OK? Go ahead. She'll meet you there."

Whitey hopped out of the huddle and jogged off.

"I'm a little nervous," I confessed.

"About this? *One Mississippi, two Mississippi*—don't be a pussy—*four Mississippi….* Didn't you ever take a girl out on a date before?"

I thought for a moment. "No."

"Well, this'll be good practice—at least for the stopping-up part."

I looked toward Goldfarb's Guest House, which looked serene in the lull of the after-dinner hour. It bothered me that the people inside were so unaware that they were about to become the victims of a secret mission. But it bothered me more that I had to pick up a girl. My nerve was evaporating with each *Mississippi*. I secretly wished Frankie would suddenly decide to trick Whitey and abandon the plan. That was just the kind of thing he liked to do. But he just kept counting. *"Twenty-two, twenty-three…"* He'd gotten tired of the *Mississippi* part.

Though the evening was warm, I was freezing and sweating at the same time. I shouldn't be nervous, I told myself. I'd stopped up for girls before—though not to go out on a date, just her and me—and not for someone as pretty as Ellen. Well, I reasoned, it'll be over in no time. All I have to do is stop by the house, say hello to Izzy and Mrs. Goldfarb, and get the girl. Maybe Izzy is out on a job. *What'll I say to her?*

"...*A hundred!* Go get her," said Frankie. He gave me a little push, and I marched slowly up the street.

As I climbed the flowery steps of Goldfarb's Guest House, I felt like every eye in the street was looking at me from behind every dark window. I glanced back at my house to make certain that none of my brothers was watching. They'd have something to say if they were. Only Frankie was there, and he shooed me on.

I knocked on Ellen's door. I heard my heart pound. Plump and pleasant Mrs. Goldfarb let me in. "Ah, Richard," she said happily. I thought about how silly Mrs. Goldfarb had looked the other night when we saw her on her porch, but I couldn't laugh about it now. I tried to say hello, but it didn't come out. *"Mmm-uh,"* I said. Mrs. Goldfarb smiled at me grandmotherly, which made me feel better.

Behind her, the dreaded Izzy sat in a rocking chair. He had been reading a Yiddish newspaper which he now laid on his lap. He smiled at me, showing his three teeth. I avoided his eyes by glancing across the room where, on a chest covered with a lace, a village of Hummels stared back.

I looked at the little statues for a while as the old couple eyed me, waiting for an explanation for my visit.

Oh God, I realized, I hadn't rehearsed. "Is Ellen home?" I asked.

Relieved, Mrs. Goldfarb said, "I'll get her," and she creaked up the stairs, leaving me alone with Izzy.

I moved just inside the room and looked at the Oriental carpet. In each corner of the carpet a fire breathing dragon circled a globe.

"So vy don't you sit?" said Izzy. He seemed jolly, flashing his gummy smile and pointing to a chair near his.

I dared not sit. I looked past Izzy at a large brass samovar gleaming on a mahogany table. "No...no...no.... That's OK," I said. "I can wait here."

Izzy put his paper aside and chuckled. "So, Richid, you are goink mit Ellen on a walk? Dot's nice. You're a goot boy. I always taught you wuz a goot boy." A broader, gummier smile.

I was too weak to smile back.

"You know, I remember ven you vas a little baby. I helt you in mine arms, and you cried to look at me. You tought I vas de ugliest t'ink in de vorld." He laughed, wrinkling his whole face. I tried to laugh along but couldn't raise more than a weak grin. Ordinarily, I would have allowed myself a good inner giggle at Izzy's pruny face. But under the circumstances, even though he was joking around, he seemed serious. The sleeves of Izzy's khaki shirt were rolled up, and I could see the awful numbers tattooed on his forearm. I felt ashamed. I got cold feet. I mumbled,"I, I, uh…" And I was about to say that I was going to leave. But the idea of leaving seemed even worse than staying. If I left, I'd have plenty of explaining to do. I didn't want to stay and I didn't want to go. So I lowered my eyes and looked at the dragons on the carpet.

Izzy winked at me. "Dun't be nervous," he advised, "Beleef me, Ellen is prob'ly just as nervous as you. Tell me, Richid, does you mudda know you go out on dates?"

Terror made me think fast. I replied, "No, she doesn't, Mr. Goldfarb. And, if you don't mind, I'd appreciate it if you didn't say anything to her."

"All right. Don' vo'ry. You can depend on me," he said. "You know," he continued confidentially, "dere's not many boys I'd trust mit Ellen to go out on a date. Not around here, if you know vat I mean." He winked again and nodded his head.

"I don't blame you," I said.

"De udder boys 'round here iss not fit for mine—"

We heard Mrs. Goldfarb's heavy steps on the stairs, and Izzy winked at me and reopened his newspaper with the Hebrew letters.

Ellen appeared. She smiled and looked at me conspiratorially. Her luxuriant hair filled the room with the smell of baby shampoo. For a moment, I imagined that Ellen was actually *my* date, and I forgot about Izzy. I smiled back at Ellen with what was most likely the silliest smile she'd ever seen.

"So where are you going?" asked Mrs. Goldfarb.

"On the boards," sang Ellen, and she walked past us and out the door.

I appreciated the way she did that. "Bye," I said, scooting out and following Ellen down the porch steps.

I felt again like everyone on the street was watching me, but it didn't bother me this time. I was so relieved to have the Izzy part of the assignment behind me. And I was proud of myself for improvising the part about keeping the date a secret. Walking next to Ellen, although it would be just for a while, was a new kind of fun, too. I liked the looks of the little gold hearts pinned in her ears.

We walked briskly up the street. "Whitey's up on New Hampshire Avenue," I said.

"I know," Ellen sang. She was wearing a white dress with almost imperceptible red stripes that made the dress look pink, and her nails were painted red.

"How long are you down for?" I asked.

"Another week or so," she said.

I fumbled around for something to say that might impress her. "Whitey's dad's got a boat." I said, but I realized that this was Whitey's story to tell, and I didn't have the time to do the story justice.

"I know," said Ellen.

I had shot my load—couldn't think of another word the rest of the way. At the top of the street, we saw Whitey sitting on a bench a little way down the boardwalk. Ellen turned to me briefly and said, "Thank you, Richie. My grandparents keep me chained to my brothers all the time if I'm out of their sight." She tapped my elbow and ran off.

"It's all right," I said after she'd gone, to no one in particular.

I walked to the rail of the boardwalk and looked at the ocean while I waited for Frankie to rejoin me. The tide was full-moon high. The water ran nearly to the boardwalk, and the Vermont Avenue jetty was almost submerged.

I looked in the direction of the Steel Pier, where the crowded part of the boardwalk began. I imagined that if I *had* taken Ellen out on a date, we'd go that way, maybe to Steeplechase Pier and ride the Ferris wheel. Then we'd share a bag of caramel corn and talk about our winter lives. I would not have lied to Izzy.

I looked back at the ocean. The waves were breaking far from the surf, and still surging strong all the way to the beach. The flats would be long tomorrow at low tide. On the beach, toward Connecticut Avenue, three young women were playing in the rough surf. I could tell they were locals by the way they handled themselves in the waves. On the beach, watching them, sat a young tough with his elbows in the sand, smoking. He wore a sleeveless T-shirt, and his big arms were covered in tattoos. I recognized him as the attendant from the parking lot just off the boardwalk on Connecticut Avenue. When the girls ran out of the ocean, one girl ran to him and stood next to him. I recognized her, too: It was Theresa, CJ's sister, who did her ironing half-naked. She shook the water from her wet hair onto the parking lot attendant's shirt, making him flinch. He put his cigarette between his lips, freeing his hands, so he could sit up and intertwine his fingers with Theresa's. Then he bent her hands back, making her kneel. She screamed, succumbing to the pain. Her friends laughed. And so did she when he loosened his grip to attend to his smoke.

Frankie disturbed my reverie. He hopped up onto the rail next to where I was standing. "Well, there they go," he said, pointing to Ellen and Whitey sitting on a bench.

"Yeah," I said, "I'm glad that's over with."

"Whatta ya mean 'over with'?" asked Frankie. "You have to take her home at ten o'clock. We're going to meet them right here. Then we'll start all over again tomorrow night. Provided the lovebirds don't have a fight."

"Oh geez," I complained. Frank laughed. "Hey, Frankie," I continued. "See those two people wrestling on the beach down there?" I pointed toward Theresa and the parking lot attendant. "Is that CJ's sister?"

Frankie squinted in their direction. "Damn right it is. Would you look at her ass. Someone's gonna have a good time tonight. Hey, Theresa!" Frankie yelled, getting the attention of Theresa and her friends. "I'll see you later!" He made an exaggerated kissy expression, and we scurried off. The tatooed guy was not amused, and I was embarrassed. We stopped at New Hampshire Avenue where we were out of sight and sat on the rail there.

"So what do you want to do while we're waiting for Whitey?" I asked.

"Golf," said Frankie, pointing toward the miniature golf course on Victoria.

"I can't," I said, "I only got a quarter."

Frankie lifted himself off the rail enough to get his hand in his pocket, and he jingled a wealth of coins. "No problem," he said. "We'll play two games, or three."

At the end of that first night, when I dropped Ellen off in front of Goldfarb's Guest House, she kissed one of her finger tips and pressed it against my forehead before she ran up her steps. That sweet gesture provided some compensation, but I still couldn't help feeling like a sap, going through all this trouble so Whitey could have all the fun.

4.

When I have seen
by Time's fell hand defac'd

When I have seen by Time's fell hand defac'd

*A **SONNET** by Shakespeare, number sixty-four. A student of
Information Technology will like this sonnet. He will like its modular
shape. He will like its logic. He can take it apart, like a gadget, and
analyze each part separately; and then he can see how it strings
together like an algorithm. Besides, it's perfectly understandable. The
images are representational and, aside from a few antique words,
the language is clear.*

*The narrator simply piles up examples of how Time destroys
things. Then, after establishing how everything is at the mercy
of time, he concludes that "Time will come and take (his) love
away." Can't get any more straightforward than that. It's almost
platitudinous—the theme of at least seventy-five percent of pop
tunes—that love is ephemeral. But then, at the end of the sonnet, there
is an edgy couplet, which raises the poem above the level of platitude:*

> This thought is as a death which cannot choose,
> But weep to have that which it fears to lose.

*This complicates things. Now it's not simply that Time lurks in
the future, waiting to ambush our happiness. Now, time's destructive
nature invades the present, where passion and hope should reign.
The narrator finds no perfect joy in the experience of love since he
knows, even in its throes, it is ephemeral. It's like ice cream. You sit
down with a double-dip of vanilla, and it's so good you want it to last
forever. But halfway through, it strikes you that the wish for eternal
ice cream is futile, that inevitably time will come and snatch your
ice cream away, and this thought is like a kick in the ass. You cannot
choose but weep to have your ice cream. (Martinis, I recall, were like
that too.) With Shakespearean precision, the couplet at the end of*

Sonnet 64 sums up the anxiety of being human. Sixty-four is in.

Maybe there will be a Buddhist philosopher in the class who will make an argument for mindfulness and living in the moment. But I'll have to push back. I'll say that mindfulness is heedlessness. That worrying is good. It forces you to accept reality. It helps you come up with plans. It keeps you sharp. I'll say mindfulness is OK for a few moments here and there, but practiced habitually, it'll turn you into a bubble-headed dope.

I didn't notice how it got there, but there is an empty wheelchair down by the water facing out to sea, and it's been there for a while. I haven't seen the occupant. I can't shake the thought that the chair-bound person rolled himself to the water's edge, crawled into the waves, and never came back.

A short time before he died, I visited my old friend Tuck. He had been suffering from MS for many years, and he was almost completely paralyzed, only capable of moving some muscles in his face. He couldn't talk, and he had trouble blinking. Twisted and emaciated, he was trapped in an elaborate, motorized wheel chair. To communicate, he gripped a stylus between his teeth and punched out messages on a screen attached to his chair. I was blabbing to Tuck about this and that, trying to be amusing, and the subject of irony came up. I joked about trivial ironies like getting dental floss stuck between your teeth and how exhausting it can be to watch television, and I was about to stray into serious territory, and talk about the irony of love—how love is supposed to be the thing that makes you happy, but usually it's the thing that makes you sad. I began, "Take love, for example—" but I stopped myself. I didn't want to say anything disturbing to old Tuck. So I drew to an abrupt conclusion and said, "Ya know, Tuck, irony is the axis on which the world turns." And he, with some effort, smiled and nodded which, for him, showed considerable enthusiasm. He punched something onto his screen. Then, exhausted, he rested his head on his shoulder and closed his eyes, indicating that the conversation was over. On his screen, it said, "I know. I'm hornier than ever." And I thought to myself how doubly ironic it was that I was perfectly capable of sex but had no desire.

I met my wife in kindergarten. We grew up in the same

neighborhood and attended the same schools all the way through high school and into college. She was always attracted to me. Sometime during second grade, she started chasing me around the schoolyard and cornering me. She wanted to talk, or fight, or play, and she didn't let other kids interfere. She wanted to be alone with me. I didn't suspect a motive for her behavior—I was a child—but I didn't like it. I wanted to play with boys. I wanted to play ball. I ran away from her and said mean things to her to impress my friends. I said, "You smell like a monkey and run like a girl!" I yelled these things at her in front of everyone. (It's funny how all the crummy things you've done are stuck in your memory and haunt you forever.) But as we grew up, through her persistence, we became close friends. And we remained friends—and confidants—beginning in junior high school and all the way to college. I took her to the prom because I didn't have a girlfriend and she was a convenient default. She often told me she loved me, beginning in the fifth grade, and I believed her, but I never said I loved her—because I didn't. She was, I thought, too plain to love. Then, in college, I mainly ignored her. I was busy chasing coeds. But after two heartbreaks, I married her. Her name was Barb.

When I ran into Barb at school after the summer of Ro, I told her about my clumsy love affair and how badly it ended—including the laughing dog—and I thought Barb would find it amusing. But she didn't. She scowled. And then she punched me, really hard, in the chest.

But Ro was nothing compared to what came next.

After a drought of about a year, I began a relationship with an attractive young woman I met in a creative writing class. Her name was Angeli. At first she and I were classmates and friends. We ate lunch together in the student lounge, and we read each other's stories. Actually, I read her stories. She rarely read mine. She was from Caracas, and her English was iffy, so her stories required a lot of editing—which I did for her over lunch, slowly and with pleasure. The only time I remember her reading something of mine, she read a few lines and pushed the pages back to me, saying, "It's fine." During these lunches, we grew close, and we began to meet outside of school.

In spite of my usefulness as an editor, Angeli's leverage in our relationship trumped mine—in spades. She was, after all, a beauty; a stylish beauty, with a cute accent. She'd show up wearing hip-

hugging bellbottoms and a tam cocked to one side of her head, and she got attention. She was rich, too. Her father was a liquor importer, and he was connected to the Venezuelan government, so Angeli had a nice apartment in town and a car, things unheard of among most of my college friends. To get near to her, I jumped at the chance to read her stories—which were always told from the point of view of small furry animals, like hamsters—and I made a fuss about her imagination while I fixed her grammar. I pretended to take no offense at her declining to read my stuff. And I did favors for her beyond fixing her English. Whatever she asked. I hauled groceries up to her place, unstopped her drains, and accompanied her to see the action movies she loved (which I hated). I never asked anything of her. I put the Bergman and Fellini movies I liked on hold. Pretty and rich outdoes culturally sophisticated any day.

Then I struck gold. Our friendship blossomed into a love affair. I found my way into her bed. For months, we were erotically preoccupied, and this was—for me—pure joy. Angeli, I found, was a beauty from head to toe, and I adored her body. Once, I asked her how it came to be that she was so perfect, and she responded, without irony, "My father knows the best surgeon in all of Venezuela." (This said, I conducted a diligent search, all over her body for scars, but I couldn't find any.) She was something to behold. If I had encountered Shakespeare's sixty-fourth sonnet during the amorous part of our affair and read how the narrator weeps to have that which he fears to lose, I would have tossed it aside, laughing. My bliss was way stronger than Shakespearean logic.

I lived at home with my mother and brother, so our rendezvous took place in Angeli's apartment, in her bedroom—which complimented her good looks, with its overflowing jewelry boxes, and the scent of perfume and powder in the air. Entangled with Angeli in her bed, I swore I was in love. I felt sure it would last forever. And I thought Angeli felt the same way. But, needless to say, Shakespeare was right. Time will come and take your love away. And all too soon.

Our relationship ended at the same time as Creative Writing II ended. But, before that, I can pinpoint an event that marked the beginning of the end. It happened the night I took Angeli to my mother's house to have dinner and meet the family. That was the first time I remember Angeli flashing at me what I came to think of as her "stink-eye," a look of disapprobation so keen and penetrating it made its point succinctly without her saying a word. Angeli stepped over the threshold of Mom's middle-class, ranch-style house in Northeast Philadelphia—replete with evidence of Mom's obsession for ornate brocades and French provincial furniture—and she stopped dead in her tracks. Her shoulders drooped. I heard her sigh. When I invited her to sit on Mom's plastic-covered couch, she sat on the edge as gently as a bird on an egg and, as my mother blabbed about how her schizophrenic next-door neighbor kept ringing her doorbell and running away, Angeli turned to me, and there it was—that profound, meaningful, soul-crushing stink-eye. After that, by a steady declension, our erotic liaisons decreased and her stink-eyes increased. My table manners elicited a stink-eye. The way I twirled the hair of my sideburns prompted a stink-eye and a cocked eyebrow. My plaid flannel shirts—stink-eye. My reading selections—a stink-eye of reverse condescension for being effete. The way I blew on a hot cup of coffee…that I laughed out loud at the movies…my eye color (which was the same as hers)—stink-eyes all around. Once, when I had a chest cold, we were walking down the street, and I spat in the gutter. This elicited not only a royal stink-eye but the first instance of her walking ahead of me, pretending she didn't know me. I even caught a deflating stink-eye during sex.

One morning, over breakfast, at the end of the school year— when I was going to ask Angeli to join me in Atlantic City for the summer—I criticized her enthusiasm for the Pope, and she shot me the most cutting stink-eye of them all, preceded by a gasp. Then she regained her composure and acted like nothing had happened. When I left her house, she avoided my eyes; she smiled vaguely from her doorstep and didn't say a word. There was no final stink-eye. And that was the last I saw of Angeli. She vanished—didn't answer her phone or her doorbell. She and her car were gone. Just as she had never uttered a complaint in words, conveying her disapproval through meaningful glances, she ended our affair without a single word of explanation and not a word of goodbye. I never saw her again. She didn't return to school in the autumn. She was gone forever.

You'd think I'd have gotten the message from all those stink-eyes, and that I could have mustered the anger or the common sense to forget Angeli and move on, but in spite of her disapproval and my

abrupt dismissal, I still loved her, and I couldn't let her go. Such is
the power of beauty. All summer, my mind seethed, day and night,
with thoughts of her, and I did nothing that summer but work and
seethe—didn't hit the beach once, didn't go out with my workmates.
Back at school in the autumn, I couldn't study, couldn't read, couldn't
rest, couldn't breathe. I ran a low-grade fever. I went to the college
clinic, and they referred me to their psychologist.

Lucky for me, the college psychologist, an odd old woman, knew
something about broken hearts. She let me ramble for a few sessions
about how deeply in love I was and how painful the breakup was,
and she concluded that I had gone down a rabbit hole of delusion
and self-pity and needed to be hauled out of it—physically. She
proceeded with a therapy she called "operant"-something-or-other,
but which I called "smack therapy." She had me sit forward in my
chair and, since she was only four-and-a-half feet tall, she was
perfectly positioned to stand in front of me and slap my face if I
said something wrong. She asked me what I had done the previous
week, and if I said, "I went to Angeli's apartment to see if she'd
come back," or "If only I hadn't twirled my sideburns," or "I must
have frightened her by telling her I loved her," the little psychologist
slapped me in the face, hard, and said things like "Warped thinking!"
or "Stupid fantasy!" Once I mentioned that I might go to Caracas to
look for Angeli, and she smacked me so hard I literally saw stars—
and moons. The first time she slapped me I said, "Hey, whudja do
that for?" She smiled and said, "Don't worry. It'll do you good,"
and we continued with this therapy until I routinely gave the right
responses. I don't know if it was the psychologist's unusual technique
or the healing effects of time, but I calmed down after a few months,
and I was able to resume a normal life.

But I never forgot Angeli. She was too good-looking to forget.
To this day, if I see a woman—or a man—wearing a tam, I think
wistfully of Angeli...maybe in bed, looking like something an artist
might paint; or at her kitchen table, in her nightie, buttering toast;
or strapping up her sandals. Then I envision what our life would
be like now if we had married. I see myself as a wealthy foreign
grandee, fluent in Spanish, with an elegant society woman on my
arm, enjoying a cocktail at a state dinner.

...And then I feel the vestige of a hard slap, and my palm goes to
my cheek.

A year after Angeli's departure, just before graduation, I contacted Barb. I told her the story of Angeli, skipping the most embarrassing stink-eyes and avoiding altogether my unique psychoanalysis. Barb was not commiserative. She fumed. She called me a "sucker." She said I was better off without Angeli, because she didn't deserve someone like me, which was a refreshing thought. Hearing that Angeli had criticized Mom, Barb's neck turned bright red. She loved Mom. Barb renamed Angeli "The Narcissistic Bitch" and never again referred to her by her real name. "The pretty ones are all nuts," said Barb, "because they never have to deal with reality." Then, she took matters into her own hands and insisted that we get married. She said it was about time.

I consented. "OK. Why not?" I said. I was sick of love, and this was a permanent way out. It didn't seem to matter who I had for a partner, and Barb was a safe bet. Adeptly and hastily, Barb planned a small wedding. She took care of everything. She even took me shopping for a suit. We'd be married right after graduation.

Two weeks before the wedding, I got cold feet. The prospect of being tied to someone forever frightened me. I ran away. It was still the offseason, so I holed up in our summer home in AC. I didn't tell anyone where I was. My plan was to lay low, incommunicado, and let the whole thing blow over. But I relented after a week, and called Barb. The shore was dismal; I couldn't find anyone I knew; the Bluebird Café was empty. I was lonely. After a tearful reconciliation, Barb and I compromised. We would forget about marriage, and instead live together as roommates.

We lived together for twelve years. Barb was disappointed, I could tell, but apparently she thought this was better than nothing. Then she had a reversal of fortune. Simultaneously, she lost her job as an administrative assistant and discovered she was pregnant. So we got married—mainly so she and Jesse, our daughter, could have access to my health insurance.

Someone once asked me if I married for love, "No," I said, trying to make a joke, "health insurance." But it didn't go over as a joke. Apparently, it's a common reason for marriage.

Barb loved me. She took care of me. She defended me. She took my side, even if I was wrong; and if I was wrong, she told me so only in private. Barb worked long hours as an administrative assistant, and she maintained our household, too. She even cooked dinner *every night. She was what was referred to in the latter part of the twentieth century as a superwoman, a woman who worked a full-time job and fulfilled the traditional homemaking responsibilities of a wife. As for me, I got away with murder. Sure, I mowed the lawn and painted rooms, but I was not a sensitive new-age guy. I was allowed to be a traditional man whose workday was through when he clocked out. Barb's work was never done. And this transpired because she loved me. She demonstrated her love all the time. But I didn't feel the same way about her, not even after all the years we spent together. She was like a pal, a sister, a colleague, and I resented her for not being more. When she told me she loved me, I just smiled and said, "Thanks."*

And then she died. She had an aggressive liver cancer, which she made no effort to fight. I made appointments for her and made sure she kept them, but I could see she was resigned to death. She kept herself sedated with drugs. She refused to join any clinical studies. She complained when I encouraged her to make an effort. She acquiesced to death as I had acquiesced to marriage.

Barb wound up in a hospice, drugged and comatose, waiting to die. Jesse and I kept a vigil. In her final moments, Barb and I were alone. Her coma was so deep, I couldn't tell if she could hear anything. But maybe she could. I was holding her hand, which was as warm and dry as a baby's, and I was thinking that I should tell Barb that I loved her. But I couldn't say it. I wanted to, but it was too big a lie to tell a dying friend. Besides, I thought, if I did say it, and Barb heard it, most likely she'd find the strength to tap the back of my hand, indicating that she was thankful for the words but knew I was lying. Then the palliative-care nurse came to observe Barb, and she told me Barb was gone. "Hold on," I said. "I need another minute." The nurse, an old hand at this, gave me a look at once stern and pitying, a look that showed me how impossible another minute was. My knees buckled. "I did her wrong," I blubbered, tears coming to my eyes. Expert at palliation, the nurse clutched my arms and told me that she was sure that wasn't true. But it was.

The irony of all this was not lost on me: In my own way, I had treated Barb the way Angeli had treated me. One time, before delivering a painful slap, my psychologist asked, "What sense does it make to remain interested in someone who obviously isn't and never really was interested in you?" "I can't help it," I said, and wham-o,

"Ouch!" Barb could have used the same advice. Someone needed to slap her and saver her from a life with me.

Sorting out Barb's things after she died I was surprised by the number of antidepressants and painkillers she kept in her underwear drawer.

●

MY VACATION hit a rut.

Sitting on the beach with Harry and Mom was like visiting relatives. It's OK to see them once in a while, but you don't want to make a habit of it—much too boring. Harry and Mom had a routine: Finding her circle of lady-friends, Mom unfolded her lounger and joined the jabbering in progress. Harry spread his blanket off to the side. Then they sat—just sat in the sun and took a long rest. Mom talked about what ladies talk about, and Harry listened to his transistor radio. And that was it—for a couple of hours. By and by, Mom went down to the water to "wet her feet," and Harry took "a little walk." Then Singin' Sam the Ice Cream Man would come by and we'd all have ice cream, and then we'd resume lolling in the now-weakening sun until it was time to go home. Who needed all that rest? The only one who needed all that rest was my dad, who worked all week in Philly and only came down on the weekends. But he hated the beach and never went near it. His idea of a good day at the shore was sitting on the patio with a cup of coffee and the newspaper.

The second time I picked up Ellen, it was much easier dealing with Izzy, but it was a lot harder delivering Ellen. I wanted to keep her. I envied Whitey. Ellen and Whitey would disappear and play at being in love for a few hours, while I hung out with Frankie until it was time to take Ellen home. Frankie and I did the same stuff we always did, but Whitey was exploring new territories.

Boring days. Frustrating nights.

On the night of Ellen and Whitey's fourth or fifth secret meeting, Frankie informed me that he knew where the lovers went to be alone. "Do ya wanna spy on them?" he asked. He had that familiar twinkle in his eye.

"That's not right," I said.

"OK," said Frank.

"Let's go," I said.

"Wait until it gets a little darker."

When it was dark enough, Frankie led me quietly into the alley behind the apartment building where Big Ned lived. This building was taller than the houses on Vermont Avenue, so sometimes, on a clear day, we climbed the back steps up to the roof to enjoy a panoramic view of the inlet. You could see the shape of the tip of Atlantic City from here, with Brigantine across the bay and the vast ocean beyond.

Frankie put his finger to his lips before we started up the steps. Then we tiptoed all the way up, trying not to creak. At the roof, Frankie peeked first, peering over the eaves. He looked back at me and almost laughed but held it in. Then he signaled for me to take a look. We carefully changed positions. I peeked, but I wished I hadn't. Ellen and Whitey were kissing. But they weren't just friendly kissing, or even affectionately kissing; they were deeply kissing—like in the movies! Where had they learned to do that? Ellen reclined in Whitey's arms, and they kissed for a long minute. And after kissing, they looked up at a full moon and its reflection on the ocean.

Frankie pulled me away. "C'mon, you pervert," he whispered, and we retreated quietly, pausing at the bottom step.

"They were kissing," I said.

"Yeah," said Frankie, "but I bet that's all they do."

"Are you sure?"

"Definitely. I can tell."

"How?"

Frank shrugged.

"Have you ever done it with a girl?"

"Done what?" Frankie teased.

"You know, everything."

"Loads of times," he said. "If you want to get laid, just let me know. I'll fix you up with one of CJ's sisters."

He seemed serious. "Which one?" I asked. Marie flashed into my mind's eye.

"Take your pick. They're all just as easy, even the little one," said Frankie, and he laughed like it was a big joke, even though CJ's tiny sister couldn't have been more than six or seven years old. I didn't like where this conversation was going.

As we left the alley I asked, "Where is CJ, anyhow?"

"He found a job," said Frankie.

"A job! But he's only twelve."

"He's fourteen."

"Fourteen! What's he doing?"

"Working at the fruit store on South Carolina."

Frankie and I spent the remainder of that night playing pinball at Wolfie's Arcade, but thoughts of Whitey and Ellen kissing nagged at me so badly I couldn't concentrate, and Frankie beat me at Rollercoaster, my best game. I felt like I needed to quit being Whitey's proxy, and I told Frankie so. But he didn't take me seriously, and I didn't either.

My days on the beach with Mom and Harry and my nights bearding for Whitey were eating up the summer, which was short enough as it was. I needed to push Mom to reduce my sentence, and Ellen couldn't go home soon enough.

THE PERFECT moment to approach Mom came the next day in the late afternoon while Harry was off on his little walk and Mom's lady friends were in the ocean wetting their feet without her. Mom was just about to doze off in her chair when I announced, "I'm bored." It was illegal to be bored in Atlantic City, so Mom's eyes opened.

"What do you mean, you're bored?" asked Mom.

"There's nothing to do on this beach," I complained.

"You've got the whole ocean to swim in, and the whole beach to play on. So how is there nothing to do?"

"Mom, I'm twelve years old, I don't play on the beach. Digging holes in the sand doesn't do it for me anymore. I want to go to the jetty. I want to ride my bike. I want to swim with my friends. No offense, but your lady friends are not all that interesting."

Mom softened. Deep in her heart she knew that her lady friends were so dull that they could hinder a child's normal development. "Oy, these ladies," said Mom, waving them away.

"They're driving me nuts."

"So why doesn't your brother get bored?" Mom asked.

"Who? Harry? He can't ride a bike, he can't swim, and he doesn't have friends. His life is inside the radio and the newspaper. It doesn't matter where he is."

"Why don't you go and take a swim," Mom suggested.

"I'll tell you what," I offered, "Frankie and Whitey and Ned are right over on the next beach. I can see them from here. Let me go swimming with them, and I promise I won't go any further than the

Oriental Avenue jetty."

Mom fell silent.

"Please," I urged.

Mom relented. "No bikes," she said.

"No bikes," I promised. "My bike is locked up at home."

"No Captain Starns."

"I won't go past the jetty," I swore. And to sweeten the deal, I volunteered to report back in an hour.

"Go ahead," she said finally, "but if you get in any trouble with those bums of yours, you'll never see them again."

"I'm a good boy. You can trust me," I reassured her. "I won't do anything wrong," and I was off before I finished the sentence.

When I joined my friends, they were lying together at the top of the beach in the hot sand mapping out a plan to build a system of canals and sand castles on the flat sand by the edge of the water. I joined them, flopping down and hugging a comforting mound of hot sand to my chest.

"You've been sprung," said Frankie, sand on his eyelashes.

"On probation," I said.

"Y'wanna help us build a city?" asked Ned, who looked too old to talk about sand castles, but wasn't.

"Sure."

We went down to the water. The tide was just coming in so we had plenty of flat sand left over from low tide. We found some big clam shells to use as shovels and, as we dug the tunnels that would carry the water from the ocean into our waterway, I hoped my mom would not look this way and see that we were playing on the beach in the same way as she had suggested and I had declined. We constructed an intricate system of canals, attracting most of the younger kids on the beach who brought their toy buckets and shovels and pitched in. An older kid with Down syndrome was interested in the project and, all smiles, he galloped around the periphery of our work, first clockwise then counterclockwise, singing something. Amid the canals, we built drip castles by mixing sand and water in some kid's bucket and dripping the mixture from our fingertips to make pointed mounds. We created an impressive city of drip castles and canals, with water that ran more swiftly through the canals as the tide came in.

While we worked, I noticed Whitey was in a bad mood. He didn't say much, and he dug very little. Mostly he drew patterns in the sand with a shard of clam shell. Why should he be glum? I thought. If I were Whitey, all set to see Ellen later in the evening, I would have the strength to build great cities of sand. But he was moping.

To get to the bottom of it, I asked, "How's Chip?"

"OK, I guess. He's got a little fever. My dad's home this morning, so he's taking care of him."

"Gonna see Ellen tonight?" I asked.

"Yeah," he said, but not enthusiastically.

When we finished the sand-city, we donated it to the excited little kids and the Down syndrome guy, and we ran into the water to get clean and catch some waves. While we were bobbing in the deep water, waiting for the next set of waves to swell, Whitey made a surprising suggestion. "Let's jump off," he said. "It looks like a good day for jumping off."

We didn't respond right away. "Jumping off" was short for "jumping off the boardwalk," and this was an activity that required consideration. It was a sport practiced where the boardwalk turned at Oriental Avenue and, instead of running along the beach, stretched over the ocean. It involved climbing over the boardwalk rail—high above a cove—and jumping. What made the sport worthy of pause was that the boardwalk, at Oriental, was about forty feet above the water, and when the tide was highest the water below was only about ten feet deep.

There was a sign attached to the rail where kids jumped that said No Diving or Swimming by Order of the Atlantic City Police Department, but the sign didn't deter jumpers; it only served to mark the spot where there was a dangerous hazard directly below. Beneath the sign, under the surface of the water, there were some large concrete pillars, the vestige of some old construction. These pillars were broken, and rusted rebars stuck out. You could see these pillars clearly at low tide, looking like the killers that they were, but at high tide you could only see their shadows waving beneath the surface, and then only when the ocean was clear. The only time you could "jump off" was when the hazard was least visible, at high tide, when the cove was deep enough for diving, and the only way to avoid jumping to your death into this tangle of concrete and rusted metal was to respect the No Diving sign and jump off to the left of the sign. The invisible hazard, and the great height of the dive, made "jumping off" a real test of courage. So we looked at Whitey without saying a word when he made his proposal, and then we looked at each other.

Frankie spoke first. "Do you think the tide is high enough?" Frankie was the only one of us who had ever jumped off. He said he'd jumped "lots of times."

"Definitely," responded Whitey. "It's plenty high, and getting higher."

I felt like saying, *"Sorry guys, my mom expects me back soon. So, later...."* But you couldn't be so dismissive of a thing like jumping off. If someone challenged you to "jump off," you had to do it. In fact, among some groups of Inlet kids, jumping off was more than just a challenge—it was a rite of passage and the center of their summer culture. Around Dewy Beach, if you hadn't jumped off by the time you were nine or ten, the other kids would force you to do it, or else you'd be ostracized. You either jumped off or you didn't swim at Dewy Beach. I'd seen that Dewy Beach crowd swinging little kids no older than Chip over the rail—with a one-two-three heave-ho. The Dewy crowd was out there jumping off at every high tide. Girls and boys.

I surprised myself by volunteering first, "I'll go." And I felt good about my decision. It had to be done sooner or later.

"I can't go," said Big Ned. "Got a game."

"You pussy!" snapped Frankie, but Big Ned glowered at him, and Frankie didn't push it.

"We're going to jump off!" Whitey decided, and we caught the next wave and body-surfed ashore, screaming, "Aghhh! Jump off! Aghhhh! Jump off!" on the way in. As Big Ned lumbered off toward home, we stepped lively toward the jumping-off spot.

On the way to Oriental Avenue, I kidded myself: *At least I'm not disobeying my mother and going past the jetty.* Of course, if she knew I were jumping off the boardwalk, she'd disown me. She had specifically said this one evening a few years ago at dinner when I had first seen kids practicing this sport and told her what I'd seen.

"Oy!" she said, "They're crazy! If I ever hear you've done that, you can find another place to live, kiddo." And she didn't even know about the hazard.

The Oriental Avenue Jetty was shaped like a Y. We walked down the stem of the Y to the point where the branches of the Y met. There was a cove between the branches, and the jumping-off spot was on the boardwalk above the cove. Nearing the cove, we could see a crowd of noisy kids on the boardwalk lining up to climb over the rail and fling themselves into the water below. In the cove, the recent jumpers swam toward the jetty—avoiding the hazard—to start their climb toward another jump.

We stopped to study the various jumping-off techniques. Most kids jumped feet first, holding their noses. The more experienced divers dove head first—even climbing to the top of the boardwalk rail and swan-diving—heedless that the water below was pretty shallow. Some smaller kids hesitated, mustering the courage to jump. They were on the ocean side of the rail, but they held on for dear life as they looked fearfully down. And then there were those who needed to be tossed over the rails—mainly girls who shrieked and pretended to resist. But everyone respected the NO DIVING sign and kept clear of the hazard.

"Well," said Whitey, "let's get baptized." He walked ahead.

I took a deep breath and said, "I'm ready."

Then we were surprised by the voice of Big Ned, who had caught up to us while we were watching the jumpers. "I decided to take one jump before I go home," he said. He realized he couldn't face us tomorrow if we had all "jumped off" and he hadn't.

We walked silently toward the boardwalk. Then Frankie looked at the gaggle of jumpers, "Hey, look," he said. "There's Louie Potts." He pointed to a skinny kid with long hair whose back was bent like a cobra's. "Ya know what? He jerked off so much his dick turned black."

"That's not true," I said.

"Is too," said Frankie, "I seen it in gym class. His dick's jet black. Tell him, Whitey."

"Don't look at me," said Whitey. "My dick's as pink as bubblegum, so I must not be doing it enough."

That cracked us all up, especially Ned.

We walked slowly to the place where we could climb onto the boardwalk and join the jumpers. When we got close to a good jumping-off spot, I was swept into the swarm of kids crowding the rail, and I lost track of my friends. The boardwalk was slippery, drenched from all the activity of the jumpers. I found myself in an unruly gaggle, pushed toward the rail and then pressed up against it. My turn had come. The swaying water in the cove below looked like it was a hundred feet away. I slipped through the rail and became one of those fearful kids who hesitates on the ocean side, looking down and holding tight. The water was choppy and opaque, hiding everything that lurked beneath. I heard the waves dashing against the sea-wall behind the boardwalk. I felt dizzy. I looked to my side to make sure I wasn't near the NO DIVING sign, and there, very close to the sign was Whitey, clinging to the rail just like me. "C'mon! Jump!" shouted the kids behind me. I knew if I waited any longer they'd push me. So I held my nose and jumped. The world shot up. There was a splash and the roar of water in my ears. Underwater, I heard a few other muffled splashes. Then my feet lightly touched the soft sand at the bottom. No rusty rods had stabbed me. I was safe. I was baptized.

I met Whitey treading water when I emerged. Overcome with pride at having successfully "jumped off," all I could say to him was, "Whoa...whoa!" He smiled broadly and urgently pointed up at something where the boardwalk jumpers were gathered. I looked up just in time to see Frankie being tossed over the rail by some joyful Dewy Beach tough guys. Apparently, he'd taken too long to jump, so they gave him the ol' heave-ho treatment they reserved for little kids and girls. He landed near us, and when he surfaced, he swabbed the water off his face and said, "Those bastards didn't give me a chance to jump!"

Following the others, we swam around the hazard and climbed onto the jetty to consider another jump.

"Whudja think?" I asked Frankie.

"Not as good as last time."

"Where's Ned?" asked Whitey.

We looked into the cove where none of the heads rising and falling on the water was Ned's. But Whitey spotted him on the boardwalk among the confusing tangle of jumpers waiting for their turn. He was holding onto the rail at the edge of the crowd where the jumpers were not so pushy. He was on the ocean side, looking down, and we could see he didn't want to jump. We stood. Ned glanced over, saw us standing together, and let go of the rail. But his jump was more like a slip than a jump. Maybe someone pushed him. On his way down, the back of his head struck the edge of the boardwalk, and his whole body went limp. He plopped into the cove like a rag doll.

When Ned didn't come right up, we looked at each other in alarm. Then we scrambled down the rocks, dove into the water, and swam toward the spot where Ned had splashed. By the time we got there, some older guys had lifted Ned's head out of the water. He was bleeding and woozy. He muttered, "Gotta pitch tonight." We guided him to the shallow water under the boardwalk. From there we walked him through the neck-high water and onto the jetty.

Once on the jetty, Ned regained some of his wits. Whitey and Frankie helped him stand. They put their arms around his waist and supported his big frame as he hobbled between them. I couldn't help, because I was late to report back to Mom. They climbed unsteadily down to Oriental Avenue, and I headed toward the beach. I'd have to check on Ned later.

My mother was just waking from her nap when I returned. "Hi, Mom. I'm back," I said, seating myself at the foot of her lounger.

Harry was listening to a baseball game on the radio.

"So, where did you go?" Mom asked.

"Just down to the jetty," I said.

"And did you have any more fun than you would have had right here?" asked Mom.

I shrugged. "I guess."

AFTER dinner that night I couldn't find Frankie, which was OK since I no longer needed his prodding to pick up Ellen. On my way to Ellen's, I saw Big Ned and his family in their car heading for the ball park. Ned was dressed in his baseball uniform, so I assumed he was OK.

When I arrived at Ellen's, Izzy was sitting on the porch stuffing tobacco into his pipe. He said, "Sit down, Richid. Ellen vill be out in a minute."

"OK." I sat across from Izzy while he lit his pipe.

"So, Richid, you and Ellen must really be getting alonk. You go out mit her evera night."

"Well, sir, I'm very happy to keep her company," I said, "I know she doesn't have a lot of friends here."

The smoke from Izzy's pipe raised one of his eyebrows, "Tell me da trut', Richid. Ven you and Ellen go out, you don't mit up vit any of your friends from da neighborhood, do yuh?"

"No, sir," I said. "Those guys would never understand about me going on a date. They'd tease me to no end."

Izzy laughed a toothless laugh. "Goot," he said, "because ve promised Ellen's parents she vouldn't get near dis riff raff, if you know vhat I mean?"

"Certainly, sir."

"Dey are *goyem*," Izzy said confidentially. "In da vinter I hat to call da police on dem more dan vonce. I know dere your friends...."

"But they're—"

Izzy put up his hands, not wanting to hear a defense. "So vhere do you two get lost to evera night, Richid?"

"Just on the boards. You know, around. We don't have much time. And I don't have much money."

Izzy looked annoyed. "You mudda doesn't gif you any...? Oh, you haven't told you mudda about Ellen yet. Vat's rrrong mit chu?"

Uh oh, I thought, this could be trouble. Izzy was pretty straightforward about things and might go across the street and inform on me. "Well, Mr. Goldfarb, to tell the truth," I said, "I haven't got up the nerve yet to tell my mother. And she hasn't noticed on her own. She might think I'm a little young for this kind of thing. And my brothers would poke more fun at me than my friends, and—"

"You're a big dummy, Richid," said Izzy, smiling a toothless smile and taking out his wallet. "You know dat?" He took two dollars from his wallet. "Here's two bucks," said Izzy. "Take Ellen some place nice, *farshtaist*? And don't be ashamed of havink a goilfriend." Izzy bent forward with the bills. "Especially a goilfriend like mine Ellen," he said.

I hesitated, embarrassed. Pulling the wool over Izzy's eyes was one thing, but his paying me to do it was another. Izzy interpreted my hesitation as good manners and leaned closer, nodding toward the bills to encourage me to take them.

I looked toward my house to see if anyone was watching. "Gee," I said. "Thanks, Mr. Goldfarb." I took the money. Izzy winked.

Ellen was unusually quiet as we walked up Vermont Avenue toward the boardwalk. She seemed preoccupied, like Whitey had been on the beach. Something was up. "Wait until Whitey tells you about how we jumped off the boardwalk this afternoon," I said. I wanted to tell her the story myself, but she was not in the mood to talk. She faced straight ahead and marched, as though I weren't there. "So how much longer are you down for?" I asked.

"Three days," she said coldly. "And I'm getting a little homesick."

I concluded from this remark and from the moodiness of the couple that their love affair must have hit a snag. And I jumped to the conclusion that it was time for me to step in.

When we were beside the Vermont Apartments, I stopped and pulled Ellen by her elbow into a recessed entranceway where it was private. "Hey!" she said, shaking loose. I caught an inspiring whiff of baby shampoo from her hair. "Ellen," I said shakily, "What do you think of me?"

She looked puzzled. "You're OK, I guess."

I looked down at her sandals and the pink polish on her toenails. "Just OK?"

"Come on, Richie. We're going to be late." Ellen stepped away.

I grabbed her arm and pulled her back into the recess. She gasped. I had practiced a speech. I was going to say, *"Ellen, you are living a lie with Whitey. All this sneaking and hiding spoils your love. You should be with me. With me everything would be open and honest, as it should be."* Then I was going to kiss her. On the lips. But now, holding Ellen's arm, and seeing the look of alarm on her face, I hesitated. How could I make a speech declaring my love to someone who looked like she was about to sock me? All I could say was, "Ellen, I...uh...I...I have something to say...." She shook herself free for a second time as I stammered, "I ah.... I ahhh—"

"Hurry up!"

"That is...."

"Oh, c'mon, Richie. What's the matter with you?"

"Well, your grandfather gave me two dollars for us to use on the boardwalk. But I don't think I should keep it."

Ellen lost patience. She squinted at me. "I have a date! Keep the two dollars," she said, and she stamped off, brushing the memory of me off of her arm as though it were a mosquito.

I felt ashamed. But I felt relieved too. The shame was for believing that just because I liked a girl she would feel the same way about me. *What was I thinking?* But I was relieved because I hadn't spilled the beans about my feelings. Revealing my feelings would have been mortifying. Ellen did me a favor by giving me the cold shoulder before I could make a fool of myself.

Still, I was embarrassed. So embarrassed that, as I walked behind Ellen toward the boardwalk, I decided I'd let her find her own way home that night. Tomorrow, if Whitey were to ask me why I didn't show, I'd say that I couldn't lie to Izzy any more, that I felt too guilty— which was true—and that I was quitting this pickup-and-delivery service. I wasn't worried about her mentioning the two dollars. That would only elicit laughter.

I wandered to the other side of the boardwalk and sat on one of the steps that led to the beach. The ocean was choppy and the waves were breaking at an angle. If the ocean had been this rough when we went around the jetty in Whitey's boat, we'd have wound up in Davy Jones's locker for sure. A flock of sandpipers ran frantically back and forth, avoiding the waves. Some dark clouds edged in from the northeast corner of the sky. With my elbows on my knees and my head in my hands, I was almost ready to go home and watch *Jack Benny* with Mom.

Then I heard the familiar squeak of hip waders behind me. My brother Fred was approaching the steps, surf pole in hand, pipe between his teeth.

"Hey, little Rich, whatcha' doin' buddy?"

"Got nothing *to* do," I said.

"Really?" he said. "And Mom thinks you're up to all kinds of mischief even as we speak. How about that?"

"Just goes to show ya."

"Wanna watch us fish? I'm meeting Sarge and Roland on Massachusetts Avenue. C'mon."

"Sure. Why not."

We walked on the beach together to Massachusetts Avenue. "I feel lucky tonight," said Fred.

When we arrived my brother's two friends were already fishing in the surf. Sarge was an old guy with a craggy face and a camouflage-colored hat. Roland was a dark, kinky-haired guy around the same age as Fred, eighteen or so. Roland had had polio, so he limped. Fred waded out to meet them, casting his line as he walked into the surf and greeted his partners.

As the sky grew dark, I spent the time exploring the jetty at Massachusetts Avenue, a sorry rockpile. I found a petrified turtle—about the size of a half-ball—in the sand between some rocks. It was perfectly preserved. Only his eyes were missing. I pocketed that treasure. Then I skipped some flat stones on the rough water. The fishermen were listening to Sarge tell a funny story about the school where he was the janitor.

I couldn't stop thinking about how stupid I'd acted with Ellen and how she must have thought I was a jerk. She'd get hers, though, when I didn't show up later to escort her home.

When it got dark, it began to drizzle a little. I walked over to tell Fred I was leaving. But just then Sarge hooked a fish so big it bent his rod in half, so I had to stay and watch. The serious expression on old Sarge's face after he set his hook, and the way he struggled to hold his rod upright, meant he had snagged an important fish.

"All right, Sarge!" shouted Roland.

The fish was a fighter. It shot out to sea toward the tip of the jetty. Sarge's line screamed off his reel. It looked like the fish would take all the line and escape. Fumbling, Sarge tightened his reel's drag and managed to slow the fish. But he couldn't crank his reel. All Sarge could do was hold up his rod and keep the fish on the hook. Sarge and the fish were at a standoff for quite a while. In the lights from Garden Pier, I could see Sarge's taut monofilament dripping in the mist and running circles through the water as it traced the path of the panicking fish. Sarge arched backwards, and his rod bent so much it looked like it was ready to break.

Fred and Roland asked Sarge if he needed help, but Sarge clamped his teeth tighter on his pipe and declined.

Sarge and his fish remained deadlocked a long time. He dug his heels into the sand and let the fish swim around crazily for what seemed like fifteen minutes. Occasionally, he was able to pull up his rod and reel in some slack. And he managed to walk backward a few yards. His strategy was to outlast the fish by standing his ground until the fish got tired. Every time the fish weakened, Sarge pulled his rod back and reeled in as much line as he could.

Then, when Sarge was dragging the fish into the breakers, it shot back out to sea with newfound strength, taking Sarge's line again. Sarge looked drained; he was breathing heavy. I thought he might quit, but he held fast and cursed the fish with every pull of his rod. Finally, the fish went as limp as a pile of seaweed and Sarge hauled him in.

It was a rockfish, the biggest I'd ever seen. As Sarge sat on the beach filling his pipe, exhausted and talking to himself, Fred, Roland, and I examined the fish in the light from the pier. It's body reflected a rainbow of color, even in the dim light. Distinctive black lines as thick as my finger ran the length of its body. It was as long as Whitey's brother Chip, and had eyes the size of quarters. It was a grown-up version of one of the little fish we'd netted in the bay at Brigantine. "Forty pounds easy, probably more" said Fred. As a courtesy to Sarge, Roland cut the fish's neck below the gills and it died.

The fishermen took turns carrying the fish to the parking lot where Sarge had parked his station wagon. As they walked, they discussed how the fish should be filleted and portioned. Mom would be happy, since Sarge offered generous portions to Fred and Roland. Sarge recounted instances of some of the other large fish caught off Massachusetts Avenue, and the three fishermen agreed that the lure Sarge used, a Hopkins, was the best lure for stripers in these parts. At Sarge's station wagon, Fred congratulated Sarge one last time and we left him and Roland.

Fred was quiet when we were alone. As we climbed the steps to the boardwalk, I asked Fred if that rockfish was the biggest he'd ever seen, and he didn't answer. "Hate, hate, hate!" was all he said. Turning, I noticed a look of ill-concealed jealousy on his face.

"What's the matter, Fred?"

"I was just thinking about work tomorrow," said Fred, but I knew what he was really thinking about.

"You shoulda caught that fish," I said.

"Oh, no," said Fred. "That's not the way it works. The fish picks the lure it wants and that's that."

But I knew he was disappointed. He had left the house hell-bent on catching that fish. And he was standing right next to Sarge when the fish struck. *Why did the stupid fish choose Sarge's lure instead of his?* That's what Fred was thinking as he puffed his pipe.

"I got something to do," I told Fred as we walked down the ramp to Vermont Avenue and neared Ned's apartment building. On the roof, Ellen and Whitey would be finishing their rendezvous. I was going to go right up to the roof and tell them they were on their own tonight.

"OK," said Fred, and he thumped off into the fog in his waders. The mist had gotten so thick it wet your clothes and collected in your hair like salty beads.

Outside Ned's apartment, his dad was sitting on a beach chair having a beer and a smoke in the muggy darkness. Ned's dad was a soft-spoken giant, always in a gloomy mood. But he looked even gloomier than usual tonight as he sat alone and stared into the mouth of his bottle. Since he was sitting in the entrance to the alley, I'd have to ask his permission to go to the back of the building and climb to the roof.

"Hi, Butch," I said. Ned's dad was named Buster, but everyone called him Butch, even us kids.

"Hi, Richie. You lookin' for Ned? He's asleep."

I heard a door swing open and some shuffling in the alley. Mr. Wolf, Ned's next door neighbor, backed through his screen-door trying to juggle a quart bottle of beer and a beach chair while a lit cigarette dangled from his lips. "Who the hell's out there, Butch?" asked Wolf. From inside Wolf's apartment I heard his wife shout, "Close the goddamn door, Chet, you're lettin' in the skeeters!" She was listening to a passionate speech on the radio.

"It's the kid from down the street," said Butch.

Wolf banged his door shut and short-stepped down the alley, where he began to calculate how to set himself up. "Oh, the little Jewboy," he said under his breath but loud enough for both Butch and me to hear. Wolf finally hit on the idea of placing his bottle on the ground in order to free both hands for unfolding his chair.

"Ain't you Jewish, Wolfie?" Butch winked at me.

"Me? A Jew? Who told you that?" Wolf fought with his chair, cursing softly.

"Why, you did. The other night. We were sitting right here and you said—"

"G'wan, whaddaya talkin'." Wolf's chair sprang open. Settling, Wolf pointed his bottle at me and asked, "You at the game tonight?"

"No," I said. "I was watching my brother fish off—"

"Goddamn most pitiful game I ever seen," said Wolf. He held his bottle aloft as if to toast the most pitiful game he'd ever seen. He took a quick guzzle. "Ned walked the first ten batters! Ten in a row, I counted 'em. Then they took him out of the game. It was pitiful, just pitiful."

I looked at Butch for verification. He nodded. "Ned had a bad night."

"That's not like Ned," I said. "Did he lose?"

"Lose? Ha!" said Wolf. "You're goddamn right they lost. They lost their goddamn pants." He looked to either side of his chair for a good spot to set his bottle down.

"Yep," said Butch. "We lost by two runs. First time in his life Ned lost a game." He shrugged and started to say something, but stopped.

"Is he sick?" I asked.

"Sick in the goddamn head," said Wolf. "I never seen worse pitchin' in my life. The kid musta been drunk or something." Wolf felt around in the vicinity of his breast pocket for his cigarettes, unconscious that he had not finished smoking the one between his fingers.

"He was all right on the beach this morning," I said.

"Well, he looked like he was cross-eyed and crazy," mumbled Wolf.

I moved toward Butch so my back faced Wolf. "Hey, Butch, do you think I could use your alley to get over to Victoria Avenue? I want to see if my brother is in the golf course."

"I thought you said your goddamn brother was fishing," said Wolf.

"That's my other brother. May I, Butch?"

"Be my guest," whispered Butch, pointing down the alley with his bottle.

Wolf straightened. "Hey, how about asking me?"

I turned and pointed toward the back of the alley. Wolf waved his hand, "G'wan, git outa here."

Walking down the alley, I could hear little Mr. Wolf badgering big Butch and Butch silently taking it. I guess he was used to it, or didn't care—"Y'oughta beat the hell outa Ned for that pitiful performance, y'know that, Butch. Yer too soft on that boy. Gawd A'mighty, he eats enough for three. Big as a house... And then he turns around and throws ten walks. What kinda—"

"Shut the fuck up, already!" I heard Mrs. Wolf holler from inside.

"Gah fuck y'self," said Wolf.

I ducked behind the apartment building and sneaked up the steps to the roof. The steps were slippery, and it felt like the fog got thicker the higher I climbed. When I got near the top, I could hear Whitey and Ellen quarreling. Peering onto the roof, I could see them through the mist sitting by the chimney. There was no view of the moon reflected on the ocean tonight. Just fog and the fuzzy glow of one street lamp. The mist had caused Ellen's hair to droop. I got there just in time to hear her speak my name.

"...You can't pick me up. That screwball Richard has to. My grandfather hates all you kids, and he hates you worst of all...."

"...Because I'm a Nazi," Whitey mocked.

"You do look like one."

"I'm Norwegian," said Whitey. "You should tell him that."

"Are you kidding? How would I start a conversation like that with Pappa Izzy? I'm not even supposed to know you. He thinks you're German, and he's not going to change his mind about something like that."

"That's nuts."

"I would never start a conversation about Nazis or Norwegians or you or anything like that in my grandfather's house. Pappa Izzy gets worked up about these things and throws fits. Can you blame him? He was in a *concentration camp*! The other day at dinner he was telling us about how soldiers marched him and some others out of their camp toward the end of the war. He said they marched a hundred miles, in the snow, with their feet wrapped in rags, and he had nothing to eat but the bark from trees. When he said he ate tree bark, my little brother laughed, and Pappa Izzy went crazy."

"Well," said Whitey, "I guess I won't see you again after Monday."

"You promised to come to Cherry Hill."

"But we'd have to sneak around in Cherry Hill, just like here, and I don't even know how to get there or where to go."

"We could meet at the mall...."

"...And sneak. I don't know. Buses cost money. I have to take care of my brother. There'd be school...."

"Your little brother is weird—"

"He's sick."

"He's imagining all that worm stuff. He's weird." Ellen looked pointedly at Whitey. "You don't want to visit me, do you?"

"Not if I can't come to your house! Look, Ellen, if I came to visit you in Cherry Hill on the sly, how long could we see each other? The bus takes a couple of hours. We'd have to go somewhere and hide for a while, and in an hour I'd have to be on my way back. What good is it? And my brother's not weird—"

Ellen moved away from Whitey. "Oh, he's plenty weird. If you don't want to see me any more, just say it." Whitey didn't answer. He tried to reach out to Ellen, but she pushed him away. "After Monday, we'll never see each other again, will we? And you don't care."

"I do," said Whitey, "I do." He reached out to Ellen to console her, and this time she acquiesced and curled into his arms.

"Plenty weird," she said.

Whitey and Ellen kissed. Then Whitey touched her breast.

I almost fell backwards. *"Whoa,"* I whispered to no one as I backed down the steps. *"What was that? They're in deep. I'm not ready for any of that."*

I walked back to the street where Mr. Wolf was still annoying Butch, and Butch was still taking it. "Y'oughta quit that job up at the hotel," Wolf advised Butch. "They don't pay you what you're worth, and you have to wear that stupid green suit. D'ya know what I told Sally you look like in that uniform? Ha, ha! The Jolly Green Giant! That's what. Ha! Ha! Ha!" Wolf raised his bottle and drank.

"Thanks for the use of the alley," I said, passing.

Wolf stopped mid-guzzle. "Hey, where you goin'? I've got some questions for you...." But I didn't stop.

It started to rain. I heard Butch and Wolf rattle their chairs shut. I ducked under a window awning in a dark driveway a few houses away from mine to wait for the rain to ease up. Ellen and Whitey would expect me soon. An older couple arm-in-arm under an umbrella walked by talking about getting home in time for a television program.

I spotted something by the curb under the streetlight. The day before, the city had done some concrete work on a small section of pavement under the lamp. Looking down, I noticed some writing in the dried concrete. It said "I Love Whitey." Ellen must have written it. How had she managed to do it? Her grandparents watched her so closely, and the writing was almost directly across from their Guest House. She must have sneaked out in the middle of the night to do it. No, the concrete would have been dry by then. She must have found a moment before she left for her beach in Margate and did it in broad daylight.

Fred was right, I thought—about the fish. If the fish struck Sarge's lure, then it preferred Sarge's lure.

I looked at Goldfarb's Guest House to make sure no one was looking. Then I turned and headed back toward the Vermont Apartments, the appointed place where I met Ellen at the end of the night. I was wet and shivering under an overhang when Ellen and Whitey showed up, fifteen minutes late.

"Oh, Richie, I'm so glad you're here," said Ellen.

"Yeah," said Whitey. "Ellen was afraid you wouldn't show in the rain and she'd be in big trouble." Whitey put out his hand and shook mine.

"Don't mention it," I said, taking Whitey's hand. "Did you think I'd leave you in the lurch? Would I leave Romeo and Juliet standing in the rain?" We laughed. "Besides, Izzy gave me two bucks to look after Ellen." We laughed again.

"Whitey told me about how you idiots jumped off the boardwalk," said Ellen, "and I told him I think you're all completely batty."

More laughter.

"We are batty," I said.

The rain let up a little. They kissed goodnight—right in front of me.

BEFORE I fell asleep that night, I thought about how I'd dodged a bullet by getting tongue-tied in front of Ellen. I felt bad about a lot of things; my naïvety, my lies, how I almost betrayed Whitey without giving it a second thought, the two dollars....

Asleep, I dreamed that Frankie, Big Ned, and I were swimming in the surf, looking for a perfect wave, a "contest wave." We had swum pretty far out. The waves were as tall as hills, and we rose and fell like buoys with each swell. Then a tall wave with a slow-breaking crest rose above me. I positioned myself, swam two butterfly strokes, and I was off on a ride that could only happen in a dream, a long easy ride with my body way out in front of the wave as though I were a surfboard, until I was beached, my chest touching the sand. Standing, I turned and looked back into the ocean to accept the praise of my friends. I held out my arms like a gymnast who has finished a perfect routine. But no one was there. The ocean was empty. The beach was empty. It was cold. The sky was the color of slate. It looked like the offseason.

THE NEXT day the sky was as gray as it had been in my dream. The clouds were so thick they could hardly fit in the sky. Vermont Avenue looked like a black and white photograph.

When I awoke and wandered into the kitchen, I discovered Izzy sitting at the kitchen table drinking a cup of coffee. He was conversing in Yiddish with my mother who was preparing oatmeal at the stove.

"So, Izzy," she said, *"Far vass is de vahsser nisht haise?"*

Uh oh, I thought, what are they talking about? Expecting trouble, I sat across from Izzy and smiled.

He winked at me and smiled back, showing his two teeth. *"De boiler iz nisht haise, Ginig,"* Izzy said.

No doubt Izzy was telling Mom about my dating Ellen. Mom wouldn't be angry at that, only surprised. But I was concerned about where the conversation might lead.

"Er denkt siz tzebrochen?" asked Mom.

"Nisht tzebrochen," answered Izzy.

Suppose Izzy was saying, *"Your son goes out with my granddaughter every night,"* and my mom was saying, *"No he doesn't; he hangs with those bums on the street every night."* Then Izzy might think Ellen was hanging around with us, and that would be a disaster.

"Veyst vas?" Izzy said looking at me mischievously, *"Richard ken mine ainicle Ellen."*

I heard both our names in the same sentence. That was it, I thought; he just told my mother I'm courting Ellen. Now Mom will want to know why Izzy is allowing Ellen to associate with us bums. Here it comes.

"That's nice," said Mom.

"Vell, ikh vel avekgeyn," said Izzy, setting down his cup and rising from the table.

"I'll see you," said Mom.

My heart was racing.

As Izzy left, Harry walked in for breakfast.

"I made you boys oatmeal," said Mom, turning with the pot in her hand. Oatmeal was not our favorite breakfast, but I said."Great."

"No 'pik'?" teased Harry, acknowledging Izzy's recent departure.

"Say, Mom," I asked casually, "what was Izzy talking about?"

With a wave of her hand, Mom said, "Who knows what that old gink is talking about?"

"Really, Mom. What did Izzy say about me? I heard him mention my name."

Harry and Mom looked at me suspiciously. "He said you know his granddaughter Ellen," said Mom.

"Whoa!" exclaimed Harry. "Nice lookin' chick!" He smiled broadly, his chubby cheeks reddening and his thick glasses rising. "I saw her the other day holding hands with Richie's friend Whitey up near Rhode Island Avenue."

I almost choked.

"Oy!" Mom blurted. "Just wait until Izzy finds out about that. He'll murder that Whitey." Then Mom turned to me. I acted calm. "Izzy will give that Whitey what-for." Mom shook a finger at me "He calls your friend Frank a *gonif,* and Ned is the *golem,* and that Whitey is a *sayna* by him. Do you know what a *sayna* is? It's a *feynt.* You stay away from that Whitey or you'll get in trouble."

"Don't worry, I don't really hang around with Whitey all that much."

"Good," said Mom and she joined us for a bowl. This was the one dish she made that she actually sat at the table and ate with us. The conversation veered toward the likelihood of today being a beach day. Mom did not pursue my connection to the Ellen-Whitey romance any further.

After breakfast, Harry and I took a walk to the boardwalk to evaluate the weather. The street was quiet except for the sound of Big Ned firing fastballs at the painted strike zone on the side of the brick ramp in front of the Vermont Apartments. Although it wasn't raining yet, the clouds were low and the wind blew strong from the northeast. It would not be a beach day. The ocean was dark and choppy, almost black, and the beach was deserted.

We stood on the boardwalk at the top of the ramp and watched Ned throw a few balls. I asked Harry why he had to go and tell Mom he'd seen Whitey and Ellen.

"You're so stupid," he said. "You think I don't know that you pick up Ellen and take her to Whitey every night?"

"Wha—?"

"Well I do. I know everything you do. Remember, Frankie was my friend before he was your friend. He and I sit out on the steps sometimes for hours after you've gone to bed, and he tells all. Mom is right, Whitey's love life is none of your business. If Whitey wants to go out with Izzy's granddaughter, he should pick her up himself. You should stay out of it."

"Whitey's my friend," I said.

"Well, it's your butt. Go ahead and keep getting involved with other people's business. See what happens."

"So why didn't you tell Mom the whole story?"

"Why would I?"

"To cause trouble."

"You dope. I hate trouble. I'll tell you what I did want to tell on you about. I'm still thinking about telling—"

"What?"

"Jumping off the boardwalk, that's what."

"You know about that?"

"I told you, Frankie tells all. Now that's dangerous. Whitey's not your business, but you *are* my business. The next time I hear about that I'm going to squeal."

"What kind of a brother squeals?"

"You moron. I'm looking out for you. I tell Mom just enough

so she keeps on top of you, but not enough to spoil your fun. And it's a problem for me, because if Mom was to find out that I knew something and I didn't tell, then I'd be in as much trouble as you. If you didn't do dumb stuff all the time, we wouldn't have this problem, would we? See if I don't rat you out if you jump off the boardwalk again."

We saw Frankie coming up the street, eating a popsicle. He waved. Harry waved back, but I was too angry to wave. Frankie hopped up on the railing next to us and sat.

"Did you hear about Ned's game last night?" he asked, pointing his popsicle at Ned.

"Hey, Frank, what's the idea telling Harry I jumped off the boardwalk? He could tell my mom, and I'd be in a world of trouble." I thought about giving him the shake-scare, where you grab someone sitting on the boardwalk rail—preferably by his shoulders—and you pretend to push him off, but instead you hold on to him and just scare the shit out of him. It was something Frankie did all the time.

"What's wrong? I thought Harry would be proud of you."

"Not likely," said Harry.

"Oh, yeah. How'd you like if I told Rita you jumped?

"G'head," said Frank, "I already told her, and she thought it was boss."

Harry was puzzled. "Boss?"

"You know, 'terrific,' 'outstanding.'"

"Did you tell her the Dewey guys had to throw you over because you were too chicken to jump?"

"That's not how he told it to me," said Harry.

"They did not," said Frank.

"Did too." Now I really wanted to give him the push-scare. But Ned had stopped pitching; he was looking up at us with his hands on his hips like our argument was distracting.

Harry called down to Ned, "So you finally lost a game."

"Yeah. Because these knuckleheads made me jump."

Frank played innocent. "Made you?"

Ned shook his head and went back to his practice. He threw a ball that bounced once before it reached the wall.

Frank said to us, "I know how to perk him up. Watch." And he hollered down at Ned, "You pork chop! You couldn't strike out Harry with a golf ball!"

Ned bounced the ball a few times and hurled another pitch. It went wide.

"Time to change your name to Little Ned. Little biddy Neddie, can't pitch a strikie. Toooo bad!"

Ned was not amused. He bounced his sponge ball two times angrily. Then he walked slowly up the ramp to where we were. I could see that Frank was asking himself if he should run away or not. Ned got close to Frankie and looked him in the eye. "If you say one more word, I'm going to push this ball so far up your ass it'll roll off your tongue."

Frankie slid sidewise off the rail. "I was only trying to help," he said. "C'mon, no beach today. Let's walk the boards."

I followed Frank and Harry stayed behind.

5.
Nothing Gold Can Stay

*__THREE__ o'clock. People are leaving the beach. Kids are cranky.
There's a sleeping guy with a lobster-red belly who should have gone
home long ago. I'll stay until four-thirty. I always promise myself
that I'll go to the White House Sub Shop after the beach and eat a
cheesesteak, but I haven't gone in years. A cheesesteak is a young
man's dinner.*

*Here is "Nothing Gold Can Stay." I need to include some
American poets in the curriculum, and who's better than Robert
Frost? Like the sonnet by Shakespeare, it's a meditation on loss.
We can slip right from Shakespeare to Frost and double down on
the theme. I can require an essay from my students with a title like
"Something Important I Lost" or "How I Lost My Innocence." As long
as I make it plain that I will not accept an essay on the death of a
grandparent—too weepy. And I don't want to hear about sex—who
wants a sexual confession from a student?*

*I wrote poetry in high school. I filled notebooks with free verse.
I wanted to be a poet, or a songwriter. Barb thought I was a fine
poet. But I wasn't. I lost the will to write poetry in college. I realized
my poetry was mediocre and, after a cost-benefit analysis wherein
I balanced the time I spent writing with the quality of the product, I
threw my poetry notebooks in a dumpster.*

*I have repeated this pattern—pursuing a literary or artistic
endeavor, confronting my limitations, and then casting the endeavor
aside—throughout my life.*

*My plan in college was to major in English literature and
specialize in Romantic poetry. I'd be a professor and literary critic.
I'd write books about my hero, John Keats. One afternoon in the
wainscoted office of Professor Romaine, my academic advisor and
instructor for Shakespeare II, we were discussing my plans, and he*

suggested that someone with my grades might need an alternative plan. He explained that professorships in English literature were highly competitive, that colleges saved money by hiring part-time teachers, and that there were many more aspirants for professorships than vacancies. He advised me not count on academia for my living. As for writing books about Keats, he explained that this would be risky business, unless I was "a bon vivant sort of chap" who came from a wealthy family and lived on a trust fund. One of the professor's elbows rested on a copy of my transcript and he pointed at me with his pipe as he gave me this speech, which was, I'm sure, a speech he often made. Smoke rose from his pipe and, like that smoke, my dreams of pursuing a scholarly career vanished in the air. I took his advice—to adopt a plan B—and I switched my major from English to secondary education.

My familiarity with Keats came in handy exactly one time per year during my tenure as a high school teacher in Philadelphia—when ol' Keats popped up in the anthology of literature we used:

> Fair youth, beneath the trees, thou canst not leave
> Thy song, nor ever can those trees be bare....

And while I'm sure my students appreciated my enthusiasm for the tragic young poet, we couldn't linger with him very long in 10th grade English. There were more practical matters to attend to—like business letters and spelling rules.

I was a pretty good English teacher. I showed up on time. I followed the rules. I did what I was told. I turned in my weekly plans and stuck to them. I decorated my bulletin boards. I corrected every paper that students turned in. I rarely took a day off. When I retired after forty years, I cashed in over two hundred unused sick days. I took my job seriously. But teaching English to youngsters gutted my interest in literature. During my teaching career, I never took a graduate-level class in literature, I avoided discussions of great books, and I never read anything outside school but murder mysteries and spy novels. I considered serious books too much trouble to bother with.

Teachers must continue their education and accumulate post-graduate credits in order to make their teaching certificates permanent and qualify for pay raises. So, early in my teaching career, still believing I had the soul of an artist, I took a course in sculpture at the art school in town—and I loved it! We worked with the human form. We made maquettes—scale models—out of clay, and then at home we worked in stone with tools we borrowed from the class. To keep dust out of the house, I worked in the basement, and it wasn't long before I was spending most of my free time down there. I spent a lot more time chiseling stone in the basement than I did interacting with my family or writing lesson plans.

Barb worried about the way my avocation consumed me. "How does this advance your career?" she wanted to know. "You'd be better off getting a degree in Education that you could use for a promotion." Barb, who kept the books for the family, was concerned about the cost of the class, too. In addition to the tuition, which was steep, there was a hefty fee for materials: modeling clay, armature wire, slabs of soapstone, and the fee for the model (a young man who looked like an attractive woman and could serve as model for either). And Barb didn't like being left alone so often. She called herself a sculpture widow. But I paid her no mind—I was practicing my art. I loved to pace around the basement, watching my creations take shape, thinking about how to solve the next stony problem, and executing a solution. When Barb criticized me, I argued that artistic expression was more valuable than worldly things, and I went on to Sculpture 102 after finishing the basic class.

I earned high praise from my sculpting teacher, Mrs. Invernizzi. She liked my work so much she referred me to a professional sculptor, Signore Solano, who she said might give me a part-time job in his studio, where I could continue my education in a hands-on way after our classes were over. I brought Solano my best piece of work—our model looking wistfully to one side—and he liked it. He liked the smooth finish on the soapstone. He called it "buttery," and he gave me a job. I assumed this job would be an apprenticeship, where I would practice to be a craftsman. But the job Signore gave me was restricted to smoothing and finishing his pieces—arduous, tedious, unhealthy work. Signore's was a commercial enterprise. He made figures for buildings, grave sites, and monuments. After my day of teaching, I would work alone for a few hours in a dusty corner of Signore's studio, rubbing away at his finished pieces with a fine rasp or different grades of sand paper until his figures were "buttery." Barb disapproved. She rarely saw me, and she hated how I often came home late for dinner with my fingers coarse and bleeding. At the studio, Signore ignored me. I assumed he had faith in me. I did ask, on a few occasions, if I might create a figure from scratch. I even offered to work for free as an intern if Solano would let me practice some techniques other than smoothing and finishing, but he pretended he didn't understand English on those occasions. Nonetheless, I soldiered on at Solano's for a few years. One spring, Mr. Solano got an important commission. He'd be busy all summer. When I made my annual request to take the summer off to work my summer job at the shore, he got angry. I had always taken the summers off, but this time Signore fired me.

Losing this job didn't disappoint me much, and Barb was overjoyed. She was pregnant at the time, and she needed some attention. She had come to despise sculpture so much, she couldn't pass a statue without gagging.

I dropped sculpture altogether when I left Solano. I hadn't the time to work on my own stuff for years and, after the hours of tedious work in Solano's studio, I'd learned to hate sculpting almost as much as Barb did.

I repeated this pattern with my next avocation, photography. Originally, I took pictures of Jesse as a baby. And I liked doing it. I still have a big box of pictures documenting her life from toddler to first grader. At first, Barb approved of my passion for photography because it was family-oriented. But as with sculpture, I got all wrapped up in photography, fancying myself an artist, and this darkened Barb's opinion.

I installed a darkroom in the basement and purchased a Mamiya 645 medium-format camera. I read and experimented. After churning out a thousand pictures of Jesse in every conceivable mood, which constituted my apprenticeship, I found my interest lay in the darkroom, where I could manipulate images. I carried my 645 everywhere I went, and if an object spoke to me (or even whispered), I took its picture. Everything: fallen leaves, rusty bolts, clouds, insects, water, display windows, people, stairs, dogs, trash cans, stones—everything! Then I went into the darkroom, made contact sheets, and meditated on how the various images might go together. When I had an idea, I made a montage by superimposing various images on photographic paper. I created hundreds of montages. I still have my favorites in a box somewhere. There are clouds in the pavement, gods hiding in the corners of rooms, bridges to nowhere, people with all kinds of things instead of heads and hands.

This process took long hours of hard work, making Barb a photo widow or, more precisely at this point, a single parent. She complained about the expense of this project and the way it consumed my nights and weekends. I liked nothing better on a Saturday night than to retire into the darkroom with a bottle of Jack Daniels and emerge ten hours later at sunrise deeply intoxicated and one image richer. One night when I came to bed particularly late and particularly drunk after a session in the darkroom, Barb went off. "You look like a zombie, and you smell like chemicals—and booze! Do you have any idea how much money you're spending on this...hobby? In one year you spend enough for a really nice vacation."

"Vacation?" I responded. "Who needs a vacation? Don't we go to Atlantic City every summer?" I was still working in Atlantic City during the summer, and we went there and stayed with Mom every summer (I installed a second darkroom there). But I knew that was not what Barb meant by "a really nice vacation."

"You're not an artist," said Barb. "You're a teacher. And you're the only English teacher I know who doesn't spend his evenings grading papers."

"I am an artist," I mumbled, falling heavily into bed. "...And I never shirk my responsibilities in school...."

"But what about us?" I heard Barb say as I fell into a stupor. After a long photographic session, I usually slept until one in the afternoon the next day.

One day at school in the teachers' cafeteria, I was showing a colleague some of my photographic work, and another teacher, Mr. Zimmer, saw the prints and took an interest. Zimmer moonlighted as a wedding photographer. After he'd looked at my work and pronounced it "different," he offered me a job as a photographer's assistant, helping him with weddings and bar mitzvahs. It struck me that this might be a good way to finance my photographic hobby. At least, it might get Barb off my back if I earned a little dough.

My job as photographer's assistant did for photography what my job as a finisher for Solano had done for sculpture—it sucked the passion out of it. The job consisted of following Mr. Zimmer around— sometimes for seventeen hours on a Saturday—and aiming a strobe light into the background of his shots. Whatever he photographed, portrait or candid, I aimed my light behind the subject. And that was it. My only other responsibility was to tote Zimmer's impossibly heavy boxes of equipment. Although Zimmer paid better than Solano, the photo job consumed much more time—so much time there was none left to do my own photography which, like sculpture, withered on the vine. My darkroom collected dust, and I traded my Mamiya for a 35mm Nikon, in case I wanted to take a snapshot of Jesse, which I hardly ever did. In fact, I developed an aversion to taking pictures. Couldn't stand it. Barb was our family's photographer during my stint with Zimmer. She used an Instamatic camera.

I worked as a photographer's assistant for Mr. Zimmer for fifteen years. Besides derailing my interest in photography, this job destroyed what was left of my social life, since I spent most of my weekends attending other people's parties. Barb, meanwhile, carved out a social life of her own, one that did not include me....

Now, writing satisfies my artistic longings. And I can write to my heart's content, without worry, and without having to compromise my art or attach myself to an employer. Ironically, my career as a teacher, which was my original artistic compromise, makes my writing hobby possible. My teacher's pension has made me, in retirement, the "bon vivant sort of chap" Professor Romaine claimed one needs to be in order to write books about John Keats. I have no wife to criticize me. I can do as I please. It's funny, though. Looking back on my teaching career, I see it—not my artistic pursuits—as my most rewarding endeavor. At the time, I thought teaching was Sisyphean and dull but, in retrospect, I see it as the most creative work I ever did and the most beneficial. Barb was right about those artistic forays of mine. They were—all things considered—a waste of time and effort.

I have learned to admire Sisyphus. I hope he has a good pension plan.

●

As Frankie and I walked off, we could hear Harry commiserating with Ned over the bad luck of his first-ever loss the night before. Frankie and I walked toward the Steel Pier, where the boardwalk was crowded. On the way, Frank performed his usual routine. He never passed the

SodaMat without getting two champagne sodas—a nickel each—one for each hand. I had a nickel, so I got one too. After polishing off one champagne soda, Frank had a free hand to belly up to the Hygrade hot dog stand under the Globe Theater and purchase two ten-cent hot dogs, which he slathered generously with mustard and relish and gobbled, saying, as always, "Mmmm, mmmm. Softest roll, softest roll." Ritual performed, we continued.

A block further, at Kohr's Custard Stand, Frankie said he knew one of the three girls in blue-checked uniforms who stood at attention in front of the soft ice-cream machines. They stood on a raised platform behind a counter with just enough room to maneuver between the counter and the machines. Like soldiers on guard, they were sworn never to speak, except to customers, and never to move except to draw the soft ice-cream or swab the counter.

"There's Siobhan, my sister's friend," Frank said. "Watch this." He popped the last bit of hot dog into his mouth and balled up the paper plate and napkin on his way over to the stand. Siobhan saw him coming and squirmed. I didn't get close enough to hear what Frankie said, but what I saw was Frankie proffering the balled-up trash toward Siobhan and, when she reached to take it, he pulled her off her platform and halfway over the counter. She shrieked and slapped Frank hard on the side of his head, which he seemed to enjoy as he pulled her further, making loud kissing noises and saying, "I love you Siobhan." I heard her threaten to tell Rita—as if that mattered.

"G'head," said Frank, knowing Rita would get a charge out of this. Frank let her go before she fell onto the boardwalk, and we ran off laughing. Siobhan resumed her sentry's stance, brushing off her skirt, straightening her bonnet and, no doubt, plotting revenge.

At Steel Pier, we noted the marquee performer was Stan Kenton, whoever he was, and in front of the Pier, we shook hands with Mr. Peanut. Frank knew the guy inside the peanut costume, and Mr. Peanut pranked Frank by squeezing his hand so hard Frank said, "Fuck! You dickhead!" way too loud, considering there was a line of little kids and their parents waiting behind us to shake Mr. Peanut's hand.

Across from the Pier, we admired the strawberry shortcake in Maisell's window. Frank stuck his mouth on the window and pressed his tongue on the glass in a mock-effort to taste the cake, saying, "Mmmmm, mmmmm," which did not amuse Maisell's lunch crowd.

We doubled back to GM's display window to look at the new Cadillac, and Frankie told me, for the umpteenth time, the story about how Whitey impaled himself on the fins of a '62 model during a touch football game and had to go to the hospital. We paid our respects to the shrunken heads on display at Ripley's Believe It or Not, and then we emerged from the dense crowd in front of Steel Pier.

"Know what?" said Frank, wheeling in front of me and capering.. "I'm going to treat you to a ride on the tilt-a-whirl up at Million Dollar Pier. Rita gave me a load of change." He jingled his pockets. "What else is there to do on a day like this?" And we quickened our pace.

I was surprised when Frankie, in spite of his jingling pockets, walked past the Skee-Ball joint without stopping; that never happened. But he couldn't resist taking a detour off the boardwalk to say hi to Ned's dad, who worked as a doorman at the Claridge Hotel. "You gotta see this," said Frankie. We walked past the front of the hotel and waved to Ned's gloomy dad. He gave us a wink and a little salute. Almost seven feet tall, he cut an impressive figure in his green livery, with his top hat giving him an extra foot. "Ho ho ho," said Frank.

At the top of the ramp back onto boardwalk, Frankie stopped short and halted me with his forearm. "There's Walkin' Leon," he said. "I have to do something."

Walkin' Leon was called Walkin' Leon because he strode the boardwalk every day, rain or shine. All day, up and back, end to end. He was a grown man—you could tell by his stubble—but he wore striped T-shirts and short pants like a little boy. While he walked, he looked at his feet and talked to himself.

"Did you ever wonder what Walkin' Leon is saying?" Frankie asked.

"No. He's cracked," I said. "Who cares?"

"Watch." Frankie came up behind Leon and walked behind him stride for stride, almost close enough to step on the heels of his shoes. But Leon took no notice, or pretended not to notice. I quickened my pace to keep up, not a little embarrassed. After a few steps, Frank shouted, almost in Leon's ear, "What'd you do, Leon?" Leon didn't answer, but he stopped talking. Frankie continued to shadow him. "What'd you do, Leon?" Frank said louder, and Leon shook his head. "What'd you do, Leon? *What'd you do?*"

Leon veered over to the rail, visibly shaken, and Frankie and I stopped to watch. He clutched the rail tightly and rocked back and forth a few times, looking up with his mouth open as if he wanted to hurl some words at the sky. I thought he might be getting ready to cry. Then he called out, "I caused three accidents!" real loud. So loud, it made the folks walking the boards give him a wide birth and stare. "I caused three accidents," Leon said, trailing off sadly and looking as if he wanted to say it again. But he didn't.

Frankie and I sped off. "Why'd you do that?" I asked. "You can see he's off his rocker."

"I had to," said Frankie, and he took me by the arm and hustled me along.

As we approached Million Dollar Pier, we heard the sound of a public address, which I'd never noticed before. "What's that sound?"

"Jam joint," said Frank.

"Jam joint?"

"Yeah, you know, one of those places where you raise your hand and get fucked."

"What are you talking about?"

"We can take a look. Million Dollar Pier's right across the boards. We'll see whose doing the pitch. Rita does their books. They know me."

"Who *don't* you know? Is it an auction?"

"Kinda."

When we reached the jam joint, we discovered the source of the amplified voice. A huge fat man stood behind a counter on wheels in front of a store that looked like an auction house. The big man had a microphone attached to a harness around his neck—although he didn't really have a neck; his head and shoulders were part of one massive expanse. He was holding aloft a little orange kitchen gadget about the size of the trumpet of a daffodil. "Advertising! Advertising!" he boomed. "Free! Free! I'm giving these to everyone on the boardwalk—free. And right now I'm gonna do it on the orange!" We joined a group of about twelve people in a knot around the counter.

"It's Cyril," whispered Frank. "He's a riot."

"What's he doing?"

"He's demonstrating a kitchen thing. Watch."

Cyril looked down from the gadget he held aloft and said to an old woman in a bathing suit, who'd moved too close to his counter, "Lady! What the hell! You got your big boobs right on my counter. Move back! Move back!" and he shook the counter. Everyone, including the old woman, laughed.

I laughed too and I looked approvingly at Frank. "See," he said.

The demonstrator, sensing the crowd was game, laughed too—a laugh that shook his bulk. He said, "When I start demonstrating the kitchen knife I might cut your boobs right off. Now move back!" He shook his counter again, and we laughed even louder.

Cyril proceeded to demonstrate the gadget, which he said was "the world's simplest and best juice extractor." Keeping up a constant line of chatter, he took an orange from under his counter and rolled it on the cutting board until it was soft; then he plunged the little juicer into the orange and held it over a glass. He squeezed, and with each squeeze some juice flowed into the glass. "You can use it on an orange. You can use it on a lemon. You can use it on on a lime. Any citrus fruit. Make a Tom Collins! A Mary Collins! A Suzy Collins! Why, the whole damn Collins family can get in on this one!" We laughed and, while we laughed, Cyril asked, "Who wants one, free?" Every hand shot up. The hand of the little old lady who was standing too close to the counter almost touched Cyril's chin. He reared back and said, "Dammit, lady, you almost stuck your finger up my nose!" And he paddled his hands at her in mock defense as we all howled.

Cyril distributed a juicer to each member of the audience, saying, "This miraculous gadget sells for $3.95 right up the street at Two Guys." And he bellowed so everyone on the boardwalk could hear, "Free! Free! Free! We're advertising today. I'm making everyone here an advertiser by giving them a free juicer! Take it home and show your friends. Free!" And the magic word "free," sailing over the busy boardwalk, drew a bigger crowd around Cyril's counter.

I looked at Frankie in disbelief. "He's giving them away!"

"He gives away all kinds of stuff."

Like a mother bird feeding a nest of chicks, Cyril gave each member of his audience a juicer, until he reached the little old lady with the boobs. "This is your fiftieth juicer, lady," he said. "Are you going into business? What a *schnorrer*!" But the lady beamed, proud to be a part of the show. Cyril had a way of phrasing his insults so they were less like insults and more like jokes.

"Are kids allowed to watch this?" I asked Frank.

"Sure. Maybe Rita's old boyfriend Joe will do the pitch," said Frank.

"Isn't this the pitch?"

"Oh, no," said Frank. "You'll see." Frank was taking pleasure in showing me something he already knew all about, which made him proud of himself, and he forgot about the Tilt-a-Whirl.

Cyril now showed the crowd a small metal blade with a screw at one end and a hole for your finger at the other. He inserted the screw into the end of a potato and, putting his finger in the finger-hole, turned the blade around and around, until he sliced the potato into a spiral. Then he stretched the spiral to arm's length like an accordion, saying, "Oh, mama! A Slinky potato!" He stood the potato upright on his cutting board and, with one cut, transformed the spiral into individual slices. "Potatoes for home fries," he said, spreading the slices on his cutting board like a dealer spreads cards. "Potatoes for potatoes *au gratin*. Look how thin these slices are!" He held one up to the light. "You can see right through it! Why, you can make homemade potato chips with this."

He never stopped talking, insulting the little old lady when he ran out of other things to say, and chanting, *"Free! Free! Free!"* at every turn. As he pushed the potato peelings from his cutting board into a hole in his counter, he said, "Those scraps all go down to the basement. When the basement is full, we move to a different location." I cracked up, imagining a cellar full of garbage.

Cyril, now flushed and sweating, rose to a crescendo demonstrating a serrated knife with a plastic handle. He held up a few knives, still in their sheaths, like a fan and explained how they were made to exacting standards by Japanese artisans. He unsheathed a knife and cut a beer can in half. He sawed a small notch into the edge of his cutting board. "You cannot destroy this blade because it's made of twice-tempered stainless steel." He brought a tomato out from under his counter and, with the same blade he'd used to cut the beer can, he cut the tomato into slices, saying, "After the punishment I've given this knife, look what I can still do. Look at how thin these tomato slices are. They're paper thin! Some for sandwiches, some for salads—why, you can cut a tomato so thin, it'll last all winter." He held a slice aloft for inspection. The little lady in the bathing suit said, "I want a knife." To which Cyril shot back, "I'm gonna give you one lady. Don't be so pushy. What is this, your twentieth knife?" Cleaning off his counter, he said, "Tell you what. You've seen this knife on TV for $14.95. In retail stores, it sells for twenty bucks. Who'll give me...a *quarter* for one of these fabulous Japanese kitchen knives? That's right, a quarter, twenty-five cents!" Every hand shot up, some holding quarters. Letting the crowd's enthusiasm build, and giving everyone a chance to fish out a quarter, Cyril continued to talk: "Now when you use this knife, never hold a vegetable like this." He held an orange in one hand and started to cut it, bringing the blade toward himself. "Because if you slip, you'll commit hari-coochie. Cut away from yourself. It's sharp, Goddammit!" Everyone frantically waved quarters now, shouting, *"I want two! I want three!"* Cyril took a box of knives from under his counter and let it drop with a crash on his cutting board. Then he put his hands on his hips and frowned. "Wait," he said, "this is too confusing. Look, I have lots of gifts and bargains for you. All for advertising. Not just these miraculous knives. But lots of gifts. If you follow me into the store," he gestured toward the store behind him, where there were rows of chairs facing shelves of merchandise,"I'll make sure every one of you gets a twenty dollar knife for twenty-five cents—and plenty more! FREE! FREE!" At which point Cyril's helpers, two teenage boys, appeared and wheeled his counter aside, while Cyril, holding his box of knives on his hip, led the crowd, Pied Piper-like, into the store. We all rushed in to find a seat. Everyone held quarters up high, and Cyril's helpers and he, good to his word, made sure everyone got a knife for a quarter. Except the little old lady, who had disappeared.

One of Cyril's helpers told me and Frankie that the show was for people twenty-one years and older, but Cyril, who recognized Frankie, told the boys to leave us alone. He said what sounded like, "They're K. Sherry and two-ten the duckets."

There was a sizable group in the store now. On the boardwalk, the crowd had grown every time Cyril handed out a gadget and chanted "Free!" Now, in the store, he began to rain free stuff on the crowd, which attracted even more curious spectators. Like someone seeding a lawn, Cyril walked the aisles and cast things from boxes into the audience. Chinese finger traps, foldable rain caps, key chains, bottle stoppers.... He gave someone a small portrait of George Washington, and he almost gave someone a sandwich in a brown bag, but one of his helpers stopped him, saying, "Hey, that's my lunch."

With each giveaway, Cyril had a joke, so before he gave out the keychain he said, "Who'd like the keys to a brand new Buick?" The crowd, drunk on acquisition, thought he was serious—that he was actually going to give someone a new Buick—so they raised their hands enthusiastically, and Cyril said, "Not the car, just the keys," and he tossed keychains all around. The helpers distributed bags so folks could store their loot, and the jokes came hot and heavy. He said he was putting an ice cream cone in one bag, and as he dropped something in another he said, "Here's some razor blades for the kids to play with." A little foreigner with a thick accent urgently stretched his bag toward Cyril for a pencil and said something like, "*Stid du va! Stid du va!*" To which Cyril responded, "Ba ba ba, shut the hell up!" and everyone roared with laughter, including the foreigner. Cyril distributed the plunder non-stop. Frenzied men jumped up and intercepted items destined for the back row; well-dressed ladies forgot all decorum, bounding from their seats cross-wise for a pencil eraser. And the audience grew.

A young guy on a bicycle, with a guitar slung on his back, stopped at the door and looked in. He was dressed in black and wore a goatee and wire-rimmed glasses. After one look at Cyril's operation, he called into the store: "Don't listen to this guy! You're going to get—" But before the cyclist could finish, Cyril's helpers were on him and shoved him out onto the boardwalk.

Cyril looked up, pissed, because he had been jabbering and joking at a feverish pitch and didn't appreciate being interrupted. He had the place rocking. So while the helpers were manhandling the cyclist, Cyril shook his fist at the doorway and shouted, "Out of here, you! Out! Out! You...you...you vision of doghead!" These words, which made no sense, seemed to make perfect sense to Cyril's spellbound audience. Vanquished, the cyclist rode off, and Cyril continued his spiel. More and more passersby saw what appeared to be a spectacle in the store and dropped in to see what all the fuss was about. The helpers put out chairs.

Looking around, I noticed there was a wide variety of items on shelves all around the store. Clocks, radios, porcelain curios, tools, coffee pots, sets of utensils, toys, a silver tea set—all kinds of things. There was a fancy looking stereo and a covered sewing machine in front of the counter behind which Cyril went to get his boxes of goodies. Hanging on the walls on each side of the store were signs saying ALL SALES FINAL, which seemed odd, since the most anyone had paid so far was the twenty-five cents for the knife.

"Why's he giving stuff away?" I asked Frank. "Look, I've got a back scratcher, a little hula dancer, and a juicer. Is he going to give away those radios?"

"Are you nuts? He's gathering a crowd. Another guy is going to take over. I hope it's Joe."

"Another guy? I like this guy." Cyril was doing a little dance while he held a tiny music box to his ear.

"The next guy is the real pitchman. I hope it's Joe."

But it wasn't Joe. A new pitchman, whom Frankie did not recognize, had appeared behind the counter, where he waited to be introduced, smoking and smiling. Cyril's chatter slowed. He laughed like a child and patted his brow with a handkerchief. Winking, he said, "Here kid. You look like hell,"and he helicoptered one last comb at Frankie. "Whew, that's hard work," sighed Cyril. He undid his microphone and handed it to the new guy. "This is my colleague, Tex," said Cyril. "I'm tired." He sighed again, let his bulk relax, and mopped his wet hair with his handkerchief. "Tex's going to have to take over. I'm old. And I'm fat. And I need a drink. Who thinks I deserve a drink?"

The crowd, which now stretched all the way to the boardwalk, applauded and said, "Yes!" Someone offered to buy Cyril a drink, and he laughed and pointed at the guy. Meanwhile, the new pitchman attached the mic around his neck and greeted the audience. Cyril disappeared behind the counter, saying off-mic what sounded like, "You should see-a-zuck my bee-a-zater for this ip-tay. Don't commop it, ya *shicker*.... God makes 'em and I find 'em...."

Tex was an apt name for the new pitchman. He was tall and lean, and he wore pointy cowboy boots. I'd never seen boots like that. They weren't leather. They looked like they were made from an animal with scales or feathers. He took up where Cyril had left off, giving out freebies. He gave everyone a toothbrush. Then shoelaces. Then Dracula teeth. Unlike fat Cyril, skinny Tex did not keep up a steady stream of chatter. He worked methodically, not throwing stuff at the crowd, but carefully placing each item in each person's bag, taking aim before letting an item drop, and slipping some of the more affluent looking customers some extra stuff, along with a conspiratorial wink. Stopping only to take drags from his cigarette, which he kept between two fingers while he worked, he made sure to overlook no one. I only heard him tell one joke while he distributed gifts, and he told it under his breath in a voice that sounded like someone walking on gravel. He was giving out pink change purses, and a man opened his bag and held it up. Tex stopped and straightened. He shrugged and dropped the purse into the guy's bag, saying, "You want a little pink purse, mister? Must be one of those boys who's light in the loafers. Or, maybe he's a *bi*sexual. My brother-in-law's a bisexual. If he can't find sex, he buys it." Those who heard the joke chuckled. But mainly Tex just moved along, grunting curses now and then and repeating "It's all free…free goods…all for advertising." Tex's approach to the crowd was the opposite of Cyril's. He wasn't jovial or energetic. He had a chilling effect. The crowd calmed, stayed in place, and became serious collectors rather than happy hoarders.

"Wait a minute. Wait a minute," Tex said after a few rounds of doling out freebies. "I need to find out who my real advertisers are." He turned and picked up a necklace that was displayed in a small box on the counter behind him. He held it up for the audience to inspect while he took a long drag on his cigarette. "Know what this is?" he asked. Someone said diamonds, but he said no, they were better than diamonds, they were cubic zirconia, harder and more perfect than diamonds. "Tell you what," he said, "I want someone out there to give me five dollars for these little beauties." The crowd was surprised. This was the first time anyone had asked for money since the twenty-five cents for the knife. And this was five dollars, not a quarter. Near us, a man whose wife sat next to him—one of the men Tex had winked at—put up his hand. Tex said to one of his helpers, "Larry, bring me that man's money and—" (aside to Larry) "—two-ten the poke." Larry retrieved the money and brought it back to Tex, who waited in silence, leaning against the counter, staring at the ceiling and smoking.

Handing the five dollar bill to Tex, the helper whispered something that made Tex's squinty eyes open. He snatched the five-dollar bill from Larry and pulled both ends with a snap. Holding the bill high in the air with one hand, he twisted his cigarette into an ashtray with the other. He placed the box and the money on the counter and paused to light a new cigarette. "I like this man," said Tex. "He's a gambler. And he's about to learn something the rest of you will soon find out." Tex snapped the jewelry box shut. Deliberately, he wrapped the five dollar bill around the box, and sent the necklace and the money back to the man and his wife. "And what y'all are going to find out about me is that I'm not doing this to make money; I'm doing this for advertising. And if you trust in me, I'll trust in you. There, sir," Tex winked. "Your money's no good in this store. Give that to your little lady." A murmur of appreciation, and some applause, went through the crowd. Tex preened. Softly, but loud enough for the audience to hear, he said, "'Stop doubting and believe,' so says the Good Book."

Now Tex took a small case of cigarette lighters from under his counter. "Look at this lighter," he said. "It's a Zippo. Best lighter money can buy. John Wayne uses a lighter like this. I should know." Tex pinched one of the cigarette lighters from the box, which required him to dangle his cigarette from his lips and keep one eye shut to avoid the rising smoke. He said, "This lighter is like Larry over there." Tex pointed to his helper, Larry. He flicked the wheel of the lighter a few times. It sparked but didn't light. "Like Larry, it won't work unless you give it a drink. You have to put some fluid in it. Maybe you've got a relative like little Larry—won't work without a drink." This joke elicited some laughter. But Tex took no joy in comedy. His jokes seemed beside the point, included because they were expected. "I've got three of these lighters up here," he said, "and I need to find out who I should give them to. Now I could just toss them out—" and here Tex feinted a toss, and a few people flinched and raised their bags. "But," said Tex, "what good would that do? I need to find people who sincerely want the lighter, who're going to take it home to wherever they live and advertise it for the Zippo Company." Tex paused for a long drag on his smoke, letting his words sank in. "I know what I'll do. Listen, who'll give me ten dollars for this lighter?" A half-dozen hands went up, and Tex pointed to three people, saying, "Ha. See what happened? That got some hands down." The helpers were out in a flash, extending their palms toward the three customers.

When Tex had the money in hand, he straightened the bills and used them to point at the crowd, "You're sure you want to give me this money?" he asked. The three customers nodded. "I don't want anyone giving me money they don't want to spend. Are you certain about giving me the money? I'm gonna put it in my pocket." Tex put the money in his pocket, and the three customers laughed and nodded. We all looked back and forth from Tex to the customers, wondering what would happen next. "Do you see that sign on the wall?" asked Tex. "What does it say?"

"All sales final," said one of the three buyers.

"OK, then," said Tex. "Just so we understand each other."

And Tex sent the lighters via Larry back to the three customers. A murmur of disappointment spread through the crowd. Tex made as if he were going to go on with the show. But he stopped, took the money out of his pocket and, as with the zirconia necklace, he returned the money, this time personally walking it back to the three men, saying, "See, that's how I find genuine people, genuine advertisers. These are my kind of people. You know, we have a saying in Texas, where I come from. It goes like this: 'You either put up or shut up.'

"Now I need an audience of 'put up' people for what's gonna happen next. And you'd better pay attention, because what happens next is gonna happen fast. It's time to separate the sweet potatoes from the mashed potatoes." He brought out a pen and pencil set in a box, calling it a "set of precision writing instruments, adorned with genuine fourteen-carat gold filagree."

The crowd was rapt and silent, so when I asked Frankie, "What's he going to do?" It was audible to everyone. Squinting, Tex fixed me in a rattlesnake stare that made me shiver, and Frankie shot an elbow into my ribs to shut me up.

Returning to the crowd with the same reptilian stare, and pointing at them with the two fingers that held his burning cigarette, Tex said the pen and pencil set would be "the ticket" for the rest of the show. "Without one of these," he said, tapping the box on his counter, "there'll be no more gifts. But if you have one of these, you will become one of my advertisers. This is where my advert comes in. I need twenty-five people to give me two dollars for one of these thirty dollar pen and pencil sets. And those twenty-five people won't regret it." Tex pointed the box at the radios and clocks that surrounded him. "My twenty-five advertisers," he said, "understand what's going on here." He tapped the box against the fancy stereo and headed toward the sewing machine. "Let me show you something." He grasped the handle of the lid that covered the sewing machine and, like a chef taking the dome off a plate of cherries jubilee, he pulled the lid off the sewing machine and said, "Someone is going to take home one of these Morse sewing machines." This had the intended effect of eliciting *"Ahhhs"* from the ladies, and Tex almost smiled. "But it ain't gonna be someone without a box. Now get that two dollars out of your pockets—pronto. *Pronto!*"

Tex told the crowd to hold the two dollars up over their heads "like leaves waving on a tree," and he sent his helpers out to collect the money. "Without this box you're gonna be an hour late and a dollar short, 'cause it's your ticket to bigger and better things."

And he wasn't kidding. After he collected the money and gave each participant a pen and pencil set, Tex stacked the money on his counter under a clock he used as a paperweight, and he turned and asked those who had not sent up the two bucks to kindly leave the premises. He made it plain they were no longer welcome, and he had nothing else for them. Surprised and grumbling, those who had not paid for a box left, disappointed.

Tex sat on the counter and took a break while the boxless people exited. He smoked his cigarette down to where it was so small he had to pinch it with two fingers to hold it. We could see the ornate stitching on the top of his boots. He lit another cigarette while his helpers organized the chairs, directing the folks who had paid for a box to fill in the seats up front. Inhaling deeply, Tex told the crowd how happy he was to finally have the group of reliable people he needed—"the cream of the crop." He joked that those who left had "tears in their eyes as big as golf balls." Everyone laughed while Tex's helpers closed the doors at the back of the store—"to keep the air conditioning in"—and Tex lowered himself off the counter, saying, "Let's do it."

A man held up a cigar and asked if he could smoke. "What the hell is that?" growled Tex, eliciting some laughter. "Oh, a cigar. I though it was a suppository." The crowd laughed. "Sure you can smoke," said Tex. "Anyone can smoke anything he likes. Hell, what does it matter? Even if you don't smoke here, you're likely going to smoke in the Hereafter. And just put it out on the floor when you're done. You're sitting in the world's largest ashtray." If the crowd had any worries when the doors shut them in, this bit of humor from the usually serious Texan put them at ease. A number of people lit up, and a cloud of smoke began to gather at the ceiling. It collected throughout the proceedings until it descended almost to the level of my head.

Tex cranked up his efforts. He gave another lucky man and his wife a cubic zirconia necklace, returning the money just as before. Then he brought a portable radio out from behind the counter, saying, "The owner of this store isn't going to like this. But what the hell, it ain't *my* father's store." Glaring at Larry, the helper, Tex took a step into the crowd.

Larry jumped from his stool in the corner where he sat, shouting, "Tex! You can't do that!"

Seemingly chastened, Tex balked and put the radio back on the counter. Pausing to reflect, he crushed his cigarette into an ashtray. Then he reached over to a display of kitchen knives and carefully selected a long carving knife. With the knife in hand, he took a menacing step toward Larry, who bolted behind his stool to protect himself. Tex, knife in hand, snarled, "Can't do that? I'll give you 'can't do that'! I'll do what I like for these nice people." Tex personified malevolence for a moment, squeezing the knife at his side—but then he relented. He relaxed, returned the knife to its place and, pointing a thumb at Larry, guffawed and confided to the audience, "The boss's son. Money and misery." Then he barked at Larry, "Back on your perch, canary. And do what you're told!"

Tex retook the radio and, walking boldly into the crowd, handed it to the guy who'd gotten the original zirconia. "Don't even bother sending up any money. You look like a solid citizen. I trust you. 'Can't do that,' my ass—I'm advertising. Who else wants a radio?" Now every hand flew up, including mine. It looked like a good radio, and for a very attractive price. "Well," said Tex, "what'll I do now? I don't have that many radios. Let me go back to my old method for finding genuine people: Who'll give me ten dollars for a radio?" This time about half the audience raised their hands. Tex said, "That's more like it. Fellas, go and get ten bucks from each of those people, and don't forget to give them a claim ticket." The two helpers collected the money and handed it to Tex, who stacked the bills under another paperweight, the box of lighters. Then Tex said he had even bigger gifts to give out—for the right people. He demonstrated a larger radio, which he said was short-wave and could receive signals from all over the world. He showed the audience a set of flatware "electroplated with twenty-four carat gold." He amused the crowd when he took a whiskey decanter, a replica of the *Manneken Pis* Brussels-boy and demonstrated how it spouted whiskey from its penis. When everyone laughed, he said, "Where did you expect it to come from, his ear?" Which elicited more laughter. Finally he showed the crowd an electric coffee percolator, "guaranteed to make the best coffee you ever tasted. Who drinks coffee from an electric pot?" he asked. And to someone who raised his hand, he joked, "Doesn't it burn your lips?" which, I thought, was Tex's best joke yet. While the crowd laughed, Tex asked "not for ninety dollars," which he said was the value of the flatware, "not for sixty dollars, not even for fifty dollars, but," he said, "who would offer me the ridiculously low price of thirty dollars for any one of these items, knowing that I'm doing this for advertising"? A bunch of people raised their hands and, as before, the helpers gathered the money, made change as necessary, gave claim tickets, and delivered the bills to Tex who, once again, stacked the bills in plain sight, this time under the base of a Brussels-boy whiskey decanter.

Without missing a beat, Tex began to demonstrate the sewing machine. He told the crowd how the Morse sewing machine was the top of the line, "better than a Pfaff, much better than a Singer." He held up a lot of attachments and told the crowd the machine could sew on buttons, make button holes, do countless types of stitches. "Why," he said, "this machine will do everything but bathe the baby on a Saturday night."

I wasn't much interested in this part of the show. There were no jokes, no surprise gifts, no threats of violence. It was a regular old sales pitch, so my mind wandered. It occurred to me that no one in the crowd had any merchandise in his hands, except a pen and pencil set and some free gifts. Tex was holding on to at least five hundred dollars—stacked under various paperweights on his counter—and he had yet to deliver a single larger item. I could feel some nervousness in the room. People were beginning to wonder out loud when they'd get their goods and what would happen to their money. Tex finished talking about the sewing machine and went on to sing the praises of the stereo.

I fidgeted. I awaited the moment when he would distribute the merchandise, give back all the money, and receive the same accolades as Cyril.

Finally, Tex finished pitching the sewing machine and the stereo. He said he needed some "super-advertisers" to take these items home. He performed that salesman routine again, saying, "Not $500, not $400, not even $200," and he landed on "the below-cost price of $150." Husbands and wives murmured. There were some terse remarks. But three people, without hesitation, raised their hands—two for sewing machines and one for a stereo. Tex's helpers shot out and took a credit card from one person and cash from the other two.

Then a great hubbub began. The helpers scurried around the room, distributing merchandise. They brought out two sewing machines and a stereo all nicely bundled in boxes with handles, ready to go. They put shopping bags full of merchandise at people's feet. Tex directed things, pointing with the two fingers that held his ninth or tenth cigarette. In a twinkling the floor of the store was strewn with shopping bags and boxes filled with stuff.

Meanwhile, the money had disappeared. I didn't see anyone take it, so I assumed it was all in the bags and boxes on the floor, returned to the audience, as the money for the zirconia had been.

Now, Tex said he had the biggest surprise of all. He brought forth from behind his counter an official-looking document. He asked, "Where are those three people who bought the sewing machines or stereos? One...two...three. Well, what I have here in my hand is a piece of paper worth more than all the gifts and sale items I've favored you with so far put together. Because what I have in my hand is an all-expense-paid vacation for two people to Miami Beach, Florida— airfare included!"

The crowd gasped, and the wife of the man sitting near us—the one who'd gotten the first cubic zirconia necklace and the free radio, and now had a set of flatware and a sewing machine to boot—clapped her hands and bobbed up and down with delight. The helpers distributed the vacation certificates.

Tex now became solemn. His eyes were glassy. He put out his last cigarette. He paused. He said, "You've been such a great audience. I don't know when I've had the pleasure to address such a fine group.... And today—is my birthday." He wiped his eye.

The crowd said, "Happy birthday, Tex."

Tex composed himself. "I'm going to give you a parting gift," said Tex. "Boys, go in the back and get that special gift for each one of these special people on my birthday." The helpers came back, each with a bag in his hand. "Go out to the doors boys. Open them up, and give one of those special gifts to each person on their way out. Goodbye folks. God be with you. And remember: All sales are final."

The crowd filed out, enveloped by smoke. Some were laughing. Some were angry. Someone said, "Well, at least it was a good show." And as they left, each patron received, as a parting gift, a post card with a picture of an old-fashioned wooden outhouse with a moon on the door. The caption read, *"Many moons have passed since you were here last. Hello from Atlantic City."*

WHEN Frankie and I emerged from the store, reeking of cigarette smoke and exhausted from trying to keep up with the show, I asked him, "What did you call that place?"

"A jam joint."

"Jam joint? But how do they make money if they keep giving all the money back?"

Frankie looked at me, incredulous. "Give money back? Are you stupid? They didn't give anything back. They kept all the money."

"No they didn't," I said.

"'Course they did," said Frank.

"Get outa here, Frank. If they kept the money, then they must have made a thousand dollars in one hour. No one makes a thousand dollars an hour. And besides, if they kept the money, it was a con job, and if it was a con job they wouldn't be allowed to do it."

Frankie rolled his eyes. "Would you have sent money up to Tex if you had it?"

"For sure. Because he'd give it back."

"Then, you're what they call a *rube*. C'mon, there's something I want to do back home."

"What kind of a thing would it be if a guy said he was going to give you your money back and then kept it?"

"I told you," said Frank. "It's the kind of thing where you raise your hand and get fucked."

"Ahhh, go on!" I would ask Fred at dinner if those people got their money back or not. He'd know. He worked on the boardwalk. "Hey, Frankie. Did Walkin' Leon really cause three accidents?"

"I don't know. Last time I spooked him he said he threw a lawn mower off his porch."

"Let's walk on the beach," said Frank, and we walked down toward the water. The wind still blew from the northeast, and the sky was even lower than before. The ocean seemed unapproachable. There were no real waves, just rolling peaks and valleys of dark water pulling sideways.

As we walked near the water, Frankie said, "We have to hurry. There's a chain I have to pick up."

"What kind of chain?"

"You'll see when we get there. You can help."

"Is it a bike chain, or a chain you lock stuff up with, or what?" I asked.

"Just come on. You'll see."

Near New York Avenue we saw a crowd gathering on the beach. We figured some idiot had decided to swim in the riptides and now the lifeguards were resuscitating him while the crowd watched. Instead, we saw a striking woman suddenly spring up above the heads of the crowd. She was held aloft and horizontal—as though flying—by a pair of strong arms. The woman had lavish silver hair, which somehow stayed in place as she did her acrobatic, and she wore a leopard-skin bikini—something unheard of in Atlantic City. We ran and joined the crowd. The muscleman set the woman on one of his shoulders, and perched there she smiled at the crowd and blew pouty kisses as the man rotated so everyone could get an eyeful of the woman. She arched her back and crossed her ankles. I'd never seen a woman so trim with breasts that big. The crowd applauded. We asked a spectator who the woman was, and he said, "It's Jayne Mansfield and her husband, Mickey Hargitay."

"Mi—Mi—Mickey Hargitay!" said Frankie.

"Who's he?" I asked, hoping I could memorize the looks of Jayne Mansfield and save it for bedtime before falling asleep.

"Who's he? You're kidding! He's Mr. Universe!"

Frank decided we had to see this up close. So we elbowed our way to the front, where there was a cordon set up in the sand to keep the crowd away from the celebrities. Like Jayne, Mickey wore leopard-skin briefs. They didn't say anything, just posed. Mickey was strong enough to hoist Jayne way up high, sitting in the palm of one of his hands. But mainly she sat on his shoulder and blew kisses, careful not to touch her very red lips. Behind the couple, a shiny new Cadillac rested in the sand. Two guys in suits—a security guard and a salesman—stood by the car. The best part happened when Jayne dismounted. She made a bouncy jump to get her balance, and then she bent and brushed some sand off her thighs. The security guy wrapped her in a gold robe, and off they went. There was applause, and the salesman came forward to talk about the Cadillac. We'd had enough of sales pitches for one day, so we left.

"Wow, Mickey Hargitay!" said Frank. "Did you see those arms, those lats, those pecs? Man!"

"Great," I said. "I wonder what it's like to be married to Jayne Mansfield? Do they sleep under leopardskin sheets? She gave me a bo—"

"Mic-key Har-ga-tay!" said Frankie, and he punched me in the arm.

"Ow!"

A few blocks from Connecticut Avenue, where Frank planned to pick up the chain, he signaled for me to walk with him under the boardwalk, where it was even darker than usual because of the bad weather.

I never understood the song "Under the Boardwalk." It portrays the area under the boardwalk as a romantic spot, which it is not. It's a dump. The sun never shines under the boardwalk, so the sand is damp and clammy. It smells rotten. Broken glass, burning cigarette butts, and dog dirt make it a dangerous place to walk barefoot. The flies are fearless—especially the little black ones that bite. They own the place, along with feral cats and stray dogs. Sometimes, even during the day, a rat will scurry by. That guy in the song who is "on a blanket with (his) baby...under the boardwalk, down by the sea" made a big mistake taking his girl there. That's his last date with her. Mom forbade me to go under the boardwalk unless it was for an emergency, like when I was little and had to pee real bad.

"So where were you last night?" I asked Frankie as we neared New Jersey Avenue.

"I went out to dinner with Aunt Rita. I told her how we jumped off the boardwalk and how Ned bonked his head."

"Do you think it's a good idea to tell your aunt everything, Frankie?"

"Sure. She don't care. She likes when I tell her about the stuff we do."

Then I got up the nerve to ask Frankie a question that I'd wanted to ask him for some time. "Where's your mom, anyway?"

"Shhhh... She's in California," whispered Frankie, but he did not elaborate because we had reached our destination, and for some reason he needed me to be quiet. "Here we are," Frank whispered. He stopped me with his hand and pointed toward the parking lot where Connecticut Avenue meets the boardwalk.

"So where's the chain?" I asked. "In that lot?"

"Shhhh." Frankie pulled me behind a cement pillar and said we should crouch. "Look there," he whispered, pointing to a big metal chain that marked a section of the boundary of the parking lot near the beach.

I looked at the chain, and I looked back at Frankie. "We're not going to do what I think we're going to do, are we?"

"What's that?"

"Are we going to *steal* the chain, Frankie?"

"No. *I'm* going to steal the chain," he said, "You're just going to help. I would have taken CJ, but I haven't been able to find him since he went to work."

"But Frankie, that chain must weigh fifty pounds. And look, the attendant is sitting right there by the entrance." I recognized the lot attendant from the other day. He was the tattooed guy on the beach who had bent Theresa's hand backwards.

"That's your job," said Frankie. "The attendant is your job."

"Whaddaya mean? I ain't gonna tangle with that guy. He's a beast!"

Frankie looked at me, losing patience, like he wished I were CJ. "Relax. You're just going to get his attention while I take the chain."

Above us, a nameless family creaked past on the boards, mumbling. A lit cigarette butt fell through the cracks. A whiff of dead fish swept by. A fly the size of a sand crab buzzed past my ear.

"I don't know, Frankie, I've never done anything like this."

"Look," Frankie said. "It's easy. Just walk up to the guy like you're a tourist, and ask him for directions. You look like a tourist. Ask him how to get to Captain Starns, so he'll look towards the avenue instead of toward me. But keep asking questions, like you don't know what he's talking about. By the time you're finished with him, I'll be gone. I'll meet you under the boardwalk at Rhode Island Avenue, and you can help me carry the chain to CJ's. We can stash it in his backyard."

"Frankie," I said, "you stole that net, didn't you?"

"Yeah, yeah. I took it from a boat. And I stole those binoculars we used to spy on Whitey. I stole them from the place where your brother works. And I stole the money in my pocket right now from the newspaper stand on the corner." Frankie took hold of my wrist and squeezed. "Are you ready?"

I tried to pull my arm away, but he held tight. "You were never a thief, Frankie. When did you become a thief?

Frankie smiled and made as if he was going to relent and go home. But suddenly, instead of changing his mind, he swung me around and bent my arm behind my back in a hammerlock. "December," he said. "After Christmas, OK? I started to steal things." Frankie applied some pressure. "Now are you ready?"

"No, I want to go home."

Frankie wrenched my arm up until it hurt. His other arm went around my neck. Another family creaked above us, this time moving faster. A drop of rain fell through the boards. "Look," said Frankie in my ear while he worked on my arm, "I'm gonna steal that chain whether you help me or not. But if you don't help, I'll probably get caught. That's the only difference." Frankie pulled up harder.

"Ow! Ow! OK, Frankie," I said. "OK. Just let go." Frankie loosened his grip. He was pleased. "Just don't take me on any more jobs like this. I'm not a thief!"

"I won't," said Frankie. "I can tell you're too much of a pussy." He let go.

I shook off the pain and considered the best way to reach the tattooed attendant. "Do I really look like a tourist?"

Frank said, "Naw. You look like any old kid. Don't forget—ask about Captain Starns. And I'll meet you under the boardwalk at Rhode Island."

On my way to the entrance of the parking lot, I had grave misgivings. If Frankie told Harry about this, I'd be screwed. Close up, I could see how big the attendant was. Dozing in his chair, he was like a sleeping bear. His T-shirt strained to cover his beer belly. Marlboros were folded into one of his taut sleeves. He had a hula girl tattooed on his forearm. With his eyes closed and his arms behind his head, he leaned his chair backwards against the parking lot shed. He was listening to a transistor radio that lay beside him on the ground. When I stopped near him, he opened one eye and looked my way for a moment, then he turned away and closed his eye as if I wasn't there. His nose was squashed like a boxer's, and he had a scar that cut his top lip in half. The radio sang:

> *...Goddess of love that you are.*
> *Surely the things I ask*
> *can't be too great a task...*

"Excuse me, sir," I said.

"Whatta ya want, Dirt?" he asked, but he didn't look my way.

"Could you please tell me how to get to Captain Starns?"

"Get lost, Dirt," he said.

I'd been called a lot of kid nicknames by adults who didn't know my name—Bud, Sport, Kiddo—but Dirt was a new one.

"But mister, I need to get to Captain Starns. I have to find my folks."

He set his chair on the gravel and cocked an eye. "See the boardwalk, Dirt?" he said. He glanced toward the boardwalk. And there he spotted Frankie who had gathered the chain and was making his getaway, ducking into the shadows beneath the boards. Frank had assumed the lot attendant would give me directions via the avenue, focusing his attention away from the boardwalk, but that was a foolish mistake.

"Hey, you! Dirt!" the attendant hollered, getting to his feet.

Frankie hobbled into the darkness, weighed down by the chain.

"Wait a minute, mister! How about Captain Starns?" I said.

The attendant took off after Frankie. Luckily, he didn't suspect me.

I should have gone straight home and left Frankie to his fate, but I didn't. Instead, I ran up onto the boardwalk, intending to meet up with Frank where we had planned, under the boardwalk at Rhode Island Avenue. I was sure he'd be smart enough to drop the chain and fly. The attendant would naturally stop to pick up the chain and, seeing the futility of chasing Frankie, let him go. I took off down the boards, ducking under the boardwalk at Rhode Island and backtracking to see if I could find Frank.

But Frankie had not been smart enough to drop the stupid chain. I could see him and the lot attendant, just a few pillars ahead of me. The attendant was gripping the front of Frank's shirt, and Frank couldn't get loose. The chain lay in the sand beside them.

The lot guy started beating Frankie with his fist, and laughing as he punched. "Here's something for ya, Dirt!" he taunted. He held Frankie up against a pillar with one hand and punched him hard. Frankie couldn't slither away; the attendant was too big and strong. He punched Frankie in the face again and again, until Frankie cried, "Stop it. Stop! You're killing me!"

Some people creaked on the boardwalk above us, talking as though there was nothing going on underneath, even though I'm sure they could hear Frankie screaming.

I thought of running for help, but that would take too long. Maybe it would be best just to wait for the lot attendant to finish beating Frankie and then help him home. But the big jerk was beating Frankie bad. When he struck a blow on Frankie's jaw that made Frankie stop moving, I knew I had to do something.

I walked into the attendant's view and screamed, "Hey, jerkoff! I know who you are, and I know where you work! Now let go a' that kid!"

He let Frankie fall to the sand in a heap and looked at me. I turned to run, but I'd got too close, and he sprang on me, growling like a dog. He started beating me the same way he'd beaten Frankie, holding my shirt with one hand and pummeling me with the other. But he was tired, and I was fresh, and we weren't close to a pillar, so I didn't get it nearly as bad as Frank had. Still, he got in some good licks, bloodying my nose and lip. Finally, he dragged me over to where Frankie lay and unloaded me on top of him. I was woozy and hurt, though I'd got only a quarter of what Frank got.

Breathing heavily and repeating, "Here ya go, Dirt. Here ya go," the lot guy took off his T-shirt and tore it into strips. I tried to get up, but he kicked me, and I yielded. Frankie couldn't move. He dragged me and Frank by our arms to the nearest pillar and tied our hands together with the strips. We were bound back-to-back against a pillar. He grunted, "This is good work. One more thing, Dirt...and Dirt," and he stuffed some shirt-strips into our bloody mouths to gag us. Exhausted and very pleased with himself, he picked up his chain and rattled it at us. "No fuckin' little dirts are gonna filch my stuff." He coughed up a golfball sized lugie and spat it in the sand. "Little dirts...." He lumbered off with his chain over his shoulder, breathing like a busted accordion. About two pillars away he stopped to light a celebratory cigarette, and he turned and said, "And if you say anything about this to anybody, I'll have to kill ya. Fuckin' dirts."

It began to rain. We heard the footsteps of people scattering off the boardwalk. Frankie stirred and started to pull at the strips, hurting my wrists. I pulled back. The lot attendant had tied good knots; he must have been a Boy Scout. He'd packed the gags in tightly too. We couldn't call for help. We were stuck there until someone happened to walk by, which wasn't likely in the rain. Blood mixed with rain and trickled from my nose into the gag. My eyes had to be black and blue, and my face must be a swollen mess.

I was angry at Frank, but my main concern was how I was going to explain this one to Mom. We might be stuck here for hours. If it weren't raining, someone might stroll by and untie us. But in the rain, the beach and the boardwalk were deserted. Our only hope was that a fisherman or a hobo or a crazy kid would wander by. We might be here until after dark. Mom would be a nervous wreck. She'd raise a search party. It was Friday, so my dad would be here soon, and if he and Mom found me and Frankie tied up, bloody and beaten, I'd have to tell them something like the truth. My dad would flip. He'd most likely go looking for that tattooed baboon and God knows what would happen. Frankie and I needed to get free somehow and put together a story that explained our sorry state, but did not include the part where we got caught stealing.

A mangy collie on the prowl approached and interrupted my thoughts. He stank, and he had patches of missing fur. Worst of all, he had foam in the corners of his mouth. He circled us and growled— coming closer with each circle. Then he came right up to me, prodding his snout under my arm, nudging me, and wanting a response. I was too frightened to move. When I didn't respond, the dog licked the blood from my face, giving my nose a special swabbing.

Apparently, the pillar where Frankie and I were tied was this dog's special spot, because when he finished lapping my face, he paced back and forth expectantly, waiting for us to get out of his way, and when we didn't, he raised his leg, and peed on the pillar, careless of our arms. This roused Frankie who mumbled some curses and, as the dog walked off, Frankie kicked him in his side. The dog yelped, then growled, and bit Frankie on the leg.

"Ungh, ungh!" Frankie wiggled, then sagged. He probably now had rabies to add to his list of injuries. But at least the dog got the message and wandered off into the shadows.

It came to me that we could blame this whole thing on the dog. I could tell my folks that a vicious dog attacked Frankie, and Frankie kicked him in self-defense; then the owner of the dog, whom we didn't know, got mad that his pet was abused, and tracked us down, and kicked our asses. Not bad. All we needed now was someone to rescue us. But the rain continued, and we could not shake loose from the tattooed Boy Scout's ties. We were soaked and sore and smelled like dog piss.

My mom must be knitting at a furious pace by now—asking Harry if he knew my whereabouts; I could feel it. Maybe she'd send Harry out to find us.

After a hard downpour, the rain let up. A big fat rat waddled by like he owned the place. He stopped to take a look at us. Frankie started whimpering. He mumbled something like, "I hate rats," and kicked at the sand. Another rat approached. Then another. They were curious and unafraid. Frank began to weep. So did I. Soon there were a half-dozen rats milling around. Frankie had the good sense not to provoke them, but one huge rat walked over to Frankie and bit his shirt, to sort of feel him out. Frank stiffened and managed to scream pretty loud through his gag.

Either this scream or the footsteps and voices we heard coming toward us scattered the rats.

The footsteps were those of CJ and his sister, Marie. They approached as though they knew precisely where we were. When they reached us, CJ stood and regarded Frankie thoughtfully while Marie leaned against a pillar.

"Tsk, tsk, tsk," said CJ, his hands on his hips, shaking his head. With muffled pleadings, we begged him to untie us, but he just put his finger to his cheek in a thinking gesture. We stamped our feet and grunted, and finally Marie said, "Untie them, you jerk." CJ gave her the finger, but complied. As he worked on the knots, he explained how "Sonny," the lot attendant, had visited his sister Theresa during the storm and bragged about beating up "Frankie Talone and some other kid," who'd tried to steal something from him.

"When Marie realized Sonny was talking about Richie, she said we had to come and rescue you. Otherwise I'd have let you stay out here all night."

When CJ removed Frankie's gag, Frankie tried to bite him, but he missed. "You sonuvabitch, CJ! Whaddaya mean you'd have let us stay all night? Ya bastard!"

"Well, you did steal his chain," said CJ.

Marie untied me. "Ew, you stink!" she said.

"I think my jaw is broken," said Frank, leaning on one elbow and rubbing his face. "Otherwise I'd have to kick your ass. Wait 'til Aunt Rita hears about this. She'll kill Sonny. She's been angry at him ever since he wouldn't help us move."

I slowly got to my feet. "Wait a minute. Wait a minute. You *know* that guy?" I asked Frankie.

He nodded.

"Everyone knows Sonny." CJ said, examining Frankie's wounds. "Didn't he work at the Seaside with your aunt?"

"Uh huh," said Frank, spitting out a long gooey blob of blood.

"Unbelievable! He tried to kill us," I said. "So he's what? Like a friend of the family?"

"He's been goin' out with Theresa since the eighth—"

"He's on my shit list now," said Frank. "I'm gonna shoot him in the ass, I swear I will."

I shrugged and looked toward the heavens, then at Marie. "Thanks, Marie," I said. Marie smiled. I smiled. "Why does Sonny call everyone Dirt?"

CJ laughed, and Frankie tried to laugh.

Pointing to some blood on Frankie's leg, Marie asked, "What's that?"

"Kingie bit me," said Frank. "And he pissed on us too."

"You know *the dog*, too?" I asked. "How about the rat?"

Marie looked around. "What rat?"

"Rat wanted to bite me."

"Again?" asked CJ.

Frank shivered. "Yeah, I hate that."

"Wait a minute," I said. "I have a problem. You guys may do this kind of thing all winter while I'm in Philly, but I'm not used to it. My mom is probably wondering where I am right now, and I'm going to have to explain how I got this bloody nose, and how I got so banged up. Listen, Frank! I don't want you to tell your aunt Rita about Sonny and the chain. It might get back to my folks. I'm gonna say we kicked some strange dog and got in a fight with the owner, OK?"

"What bloody nose?" asked Marie.

"My nose," I said, "it's bleeding."

Marie held my chin and examined my face. "No it's not. You don't look so bad. Not like Frankie. Few scratches, maybe. Did Sonny beat you up too? He's such a pig! You should see how he treats Theresa. Go down to the ocean and wash up. You won't have to say anything to your parents. You can just say you were horsing around on the beach."

"I'm goin' over your place and kill Sonny," said Frank.

"Yeah, yeah," said CJ, helping Frank stand up.

We went down to the ocean to wash our faces.

6.
Loveliest of Trees

__I SAW__ Cyril years later, selling children's wind-up toys from a little table in front of a store on the boardwalk. He couldn't pitch the toys because he'd had a stroke and one side of his face was droopy. He just wound them up and let them run around on the table. I approached him. I told him I'd seen him do his jam-joint routine back in '63, and I told him how I thought it was terrific. He nodded and said something about owning stores up and down the boardwalk in those days—jewelry stores, souvenir shops, pizza places. But his words were garbled. I smiled and shook his good hand and let him get back to business. He'd lost a lot of weight.

If I leave the beach now, I'll hit the rush hour in Philly, so I'll stay a while.

I was about to put A. E. Housman's "Loveliest of Trees" on the reading list. Here the poet sings of spring when his favorite tree, the cherry, is in bloom. He figures his life will span seventy years and, since he's now twenty, he has only fifty more springs to witness the cherry trees' blossoming. So he needs to go outside and experience the spectacle—get it while he can.

But it occurred to me that all the poems I'd chosen—except "Aengus"—were complaints about lost love and the ravages of time. All downers. I'd skipped all the uplifting poems that proved how good life is. I'd passed on Wordsworth's "Daffodils," and I didn't even reread "Invictus." I chose "Nothing Gold Can Stay" instead of "The Road Less Travelled." I'd let my own obsession dictate my choices, and I didn't think enough about my audience.

So I chucked "Loveliest of Trees." The bit about our only having a limited time to live—too depressing. And now I feel like I should chuck all my choices. Maybe not "Aengus," though I might change my approach to "Aengus."

I'll start over. A survey class in poetry should not be confined to sadness and loss, where all the lovers lose their beloved and all the poets are old and cranky. It gives poetry a reputation as a vehicle for whining. My students would likely think I was in the midst of a bummer and trying to take them down with me. I'll start over when I get home.

Oh, well. This isn't the first time I spent a day planning a curriculum only to abandon it at the eleventh hour. I'll put Twice-Read Poems *aside until tomorrow and then start from scratch.*

The people next to me are leaving. The lifeguards are moving their stand onto drier sand; the sun is slanting in from behind me. Like Housman with his cherry trees, I consider how many beach days I have left....

I sometimes meet Barb in dreams. She and I walk the landscapes of the afterlife together. We walk up and down hills, under daytime moons and nighttime suns, through nameless streets, and over bridges ornamented with statuary we'd only seen in films. Usually we wind up somewhere in the old neighborhood where we were kids. Barb looks good because she's fixed in time, while I'm nearly twenty years older. She must have found a good stylist in the afterlife; her hair is always the way it was one time when she came home from a hair appointment and said to her mirror, "There, that's perfect." She carries nice handbags too, which, as in life, she keeps stocked with Life Savers and gum. While we walk, I ask her to forgive me for the stupid way I acted when she died. Sometimes she calls me an asshole, and sometimes she tells me not to worry about it. She likes to lead me back to the old schoolyard to do the things we did as kids. She chases me around. I juke this way and that, but I let her catch me. Sometimes we kiss. We can be intimate in the hidden corners of the old schoolyard. It's good for a while, but then it turns sad. Maybe a bell rings or a voice calls out or the sun starts to set, and it's time to go home. Barb tells me that the worst part about dying is that you miss everything. She tells me how she always hated missing things, and now she's missing everything. I'd bring her up to date about Jesse, but I'm afraid it would only make her feel worse. She admonishes me for taking life for granted. She tells me I must be thankful for the things I have because they'll soon be gone. I want to say, "I'm thankful for the time you gave me," but—just like me—I think it, but I don't say it, and then I regret not saying it. The dream always ends the same: on our way home we get lost in a strange part of the neighborhood, and then Barb disappears. Either I turn around and she's gone, or she wanders off and I don't follow. One time, instead of disappearing, she melted. Her middle liquified, and she toppled over as if she were made of chocolate or tar. It was a terrible nightmare and I awoke in a sweat.

●

I WAS late for dinner. I hurried down Vermont Avenue, walking well ahead of Frankie. He had a fat lip and a broken blood vessel in one eye. His eye sockets were red and blue. Sonny's fist must have had sand on it when he punched Frank because he had countless little scratches on his face. I wished Frankie had taken another route home. This was all his fault, and I didn't want anyone to think that I was involved.

Behind me, I heard Frankie apologize—first time ever—and he promised that when he told his aunt about this incident he'd leave me out. So all I had to do was get through dinner at home without arousing suspicions about the scratches on my face. If anyone noticed, I'd say we were playing a rough game of football on the beach.

I met Fred halfway down the street. He was walking toward the boardwalk in his hip waders, seeking the elusive striper. The scent of the nor'easter—striper weather—quickened his step. He only stopped long enough to tell me that Mom was waiting for me at home, and I'd better hurry.

Entering our apartment, I eased the screen door shut. Harry sat alone at the kitchen with his head in the newspaper. The front page of the *Inquirer* showed a Buddhist monk engulfed in flames on a Saigon street. Other monks watched. Harry looked up.

"Hiya, Harry," I sang.

"Mom," Harry called, "he's home. Boy, are you in trouble."

Uh oh, they know about the chain. But how?

Before Harry could explain why I was in trouble, Mom strode in, agitated. "Oooo, you," she said, pointing a knitting needle at me, "you wait until your father gets home. How could you?"

"We were only playing on the beach," I said. But I sensed the subject at hand was not the stolen chain.

"How could you trick Izzy like that?" asked Mom.

Uh oh, this was worse than I thought. "Trick Izzy?"

"Yes, you little liar. When you went walking on the boardwalk with his granddaughter, you were giving her to that Whitey kid. Do you know what kind of trouble you've caused, you and your bum friends?" I was getting crosseyed looking at her knitting needle poking at me. "I'll tell you this, buddy-boy, you won't be hanging around with those bums any more. You can bet on that!"

"But, Mom, I don't understand. What did Harry tell you?"

"Me?" Harry said, "I—"

"Harry didn't have to tell me anything. Your friend Whitey is in the hospital and the story is all over the street."

"The hospital! Why? What happened?"

"They took him in an ambulance. Just a while ago. Everyone on the street was out there. Izzy was in the crowd and he was so angry he could hardly talk. But he told me about you and your little plan, and I couldn't believe you had some part—" Noticing that my face was scratched, Mom stopped talking and examined me. "Where were you all day, anyway? In the rain." Mom took me by the chin and scanned my scratches, even pulled my bottom lip down to see if I still had all my teeth. "Whudja do to yourself?"

"Nothing. I want to know what happened to Whitey?"

Harry answered, "He tried to commit suicide. At least that's the story that's going around."

"Suicide! That's impossible."

"Never mind Whitey," said Mom, "I'm concerned about you. Explain what your part was in all this. Izzy was too excited to explain it. He was mixing together three languages at the same time."

"Wait," I said. "first tell me what happened. It doesn't make sense."

"No, spill the beans about your part in all this, buddy-boy," said Mom.

I insisted. "I need to know what happened to Whitey. I was on the boards all day—"

Harry broke in; Mom allowed it. "OK, OK. Here's what happened. It was an unholy mess. Let's see...where to start? Whitey's little brother, Chip, was sick, and he wanted Whitey to stay home with him at night. But Whitey kept going out at night to meet Izzy's granddaughter—with your help. So earlier today, Chip got fed up and walked across the street and told Izzy all about Whitey and his granddaughter."

"No!" I said.

Mom and I took seats to listen.

"What's his granddaughter's name?" asked Mom.

"Ellen," said Harry.

"Cute girl," said Mom.

"Yes, a real beauty," said Harry. "May I continue?"

"Who's stopping you?"

"So, Izzy was angry because his grandchildren are not even allowed to talk to the kids on the street let alone fall in love with them. So Izzy went over to Whitey's and started banging on the door. When Whitey came to the door, Izzy was so angry, he started hollering at Whitey in German. Whitey slammed the door, terrified, and called his dad on the phone."

"Where was his dad?" asked Mom.

"At work," said Harry.

"He fixes refrigerators in restaurants," I said, "so he works long hours in the summer. How do you know all this?"

Harry smiled, "Ned and I saw the whole thing from up the street. First, Chip ran across the street, and then Izzy and Chip went to Whitey's. We heard all the shouting in German. And then the door slammed. So me and Ned went down to Whitey's place, and he let us in. We asked him what was going on, and he told us. We stayed with him until his dad came home. While Whitey was getting Chip settled back in his room, Ned filled me in on some things I didn't know. And Frankie had already told me some things, so me and Ned were able to piece together a pretty complete picture. Anyhow, Whitey's dad came home and went up to Izzy's to talk things over. Then Whitey's dad went back to his apartment and he wasn't happy. He screamed at Whitey for sneaking around causing trouble and neglecting Chip. Their argument spilled out onto the street. But that wasn't the end of it. Izzy's daughter—Ellen's mother—showed up in a long Cadillac, and she was hopping mad. She zoomed up Izzy's steps two at a time. She got those kids out in a hurry, hollering at them all the way to the car. Ellen was in tears because her mom was dragging her by her arm."

"No!"

"Yes. Izzy's daughter is a red-headed devil."

"Wait a minute. How did Richie get involved in all this?" asked Mom.

"I only—"

"There's more," said Harry. "Wait. You wanted to know about the suicide, right? When Izzy's daughter drove off with the kids, Whitey went tearing after their Cadillac on his bike, like he was trying to catch up. But of course he couldn't. The light was green on Oriental, and the car sped off. So Whitey turned around and sped back home—he was red as a beet and fit to be tied. He raced into his backyard where there was a clothesline stretched across two poles, and he rode right into it. He pedaled right into the clothesline, and it caught him on the neck. Almost killed him. That's when the ambulance came, and all the neighbors came out onto the street to see what was going on, and you know the rest."

"Very nice," said Mom. "Nice kids, your friends. Now tell me what your part was in this. Izzy told me you're the one who picked up his granddaughter every night and delivered her to this Whitey."

I thought of saying that my friends had forced me to get involved in this thing against my will. I could blame it all on "those bums." I could plead peer pressure. But Mom didn't deserve any more subterfuge. It was time to come clean. Harry and Mom looked at me expectantly. "Yes," I began, "I picked up Ellen for Whitey. And I lied to Izzy. I did it because Whitey and Ellen were in love, and they weren't allowed to see each other. When Frankie dreamed up the idea of me stopping up for Ellen and getting her for Whitey, it just seemed like a game. Then I did it because I...well, I liked Ellen, and I wanted to be near her. But she didn't like me. She liked Whitey. And they had an actual love aff—"

"Love?" my mother repeated. "Love?" She was at a loss for words. She set down her knitting needle. Then she looked up at the ceiling and considered things for a moment. Then she stiffened, picked up her needle, and wagged it anew. "You mean to say that you lied to Izzy, embarrassed me, got Izzy's granddaughter in trouble, and caused a scene on the street—for love? That's crazy talk. Love! You nutty kids are too young to go around doing things for love."

"*I* am, Mom, but I don't think Whitey—"

Harry broke in, "What a romantic moron *he* is. Trying to kill himself for love. You guys never struck me as the romantic types."

"Nonsense," said Mom. "He probably rode into that clothesline by accident. As for you, lover-boy, I'll tell you what. You are not going to hang around with Frankie or Whitey or Ned ever again."

"But, Mom, who else *is* there?"

"I don't know, but it won't be them. Now go and wash your face and hands. You smell like dog piss. Where were you all day anyhow? Your face looks like someone rubbed it raw with sand."

I was tired of lying. "I was out with Frankie all day. We watched the show at the jam joint, and I still can't tell if they kept all the money or not. And then we saw Jayne Mansfield on the beach, in a tiny bathing suit—"

Harry jumped off his chair, "Jayne Mansfield! In a bikini? Where?" He was ready to go.

"Yeah. She's the whitest woman I've ever seen on the beach—"

"And...?" said Mom.

"And we stole a big chain from the parking lot on Connecticut. But the parking lot attendant caught us, and he beat the crap out of us. Then he tied us to a pillar. And gagged us. Frankie got bit by a dog, and I think he got bit by a rat, too. We were surrounded by rats! We would have been there all night if CJ and his sister hadn't rescued us. And you want to know what else—?" I was about to let slip that I had jumped off the boardwalk and took a ride in Whitey's boat, but I could see Mom's patience evaporating, so I stopped short. Harry was wide-eyed.

There was silence.

Mom poked her knitting needle not two inches from my nose. "Go to your room and wait for your father," she said.

As I left, I heard Harry ask again, with more urgency, "Where's Jayne Mansfield?"

Then I heard Mom ask Harry, "What's a jam joint?"

I waited for Harry to say, "It's one of those places where you raise your hand and get fucked," but he didn't. It was the first time in my life I'd been sent to bed without dinner.

LATER that night my dad came into my room and took off his belt. I was going to get a whipping. He asked me if I knew what I'd done, and I didn't know if he was talking about the Whitey thing or the chain thing or what, but I said yes. Then he went ahead and let me stay under the covers while he tapped me a few times with his belt. We both knew it didn't hurt.

"Now, when you've calmed down, come out into the kitchen," said Dad. "You'll want to see what's going on."

I reflected for a few minutes how things you worry about often turn out not to be as bad as you thought; I'd been expecting a proper hiding. Then I climbed out of bed and went into the kitchen. It was unusually crowded and bright for this time of night. Something was going on at the kitchen table, but I couldn't see what it was because of the crowd. A night-level murmur went around the table, low enough so I could hear the bugs outside bumping into the screens. Standing at one end of the table were Mom and Sarge, each holding a knife. Mom's knife was long and slender and Sarge's was shorter and lethal-looking. Dad sat at the other end of the table with his legs crossed, less concerned than the others, reading his newspaper. Fred and Harry had their backs to me. Fred still wore his hip waders. Behind the table I could see the faces of Izzy and Rita, both rapt by what was happening on the table. Roland, also in hip waders, stood behind them, beaming. The mean lady next door, who never left her enclosed porch, was there too. I'd never seen her in the light before. She had a kindly look and bore no resemblance to the shadowy sentinel that screeched, "Hey, you kids, get out of my driveway!" Sarge was about to make a point. He gestured with the lit pipe he held in the hand without the knife.

I shouldered my way in between Fred and Harry to see what was on the table. There lay a decapitated, eviscerated, and definned striped bass as big as me, just under five feet. He lay on a portion of the paper Dad had surrendered. Mom and Sarge were discussing how to proceed with the filleting. The others looked on, likely having been offered a share.

"I'll scale her," said Sarge, "then you can use that thing," Sarge tapped Mom's carving knife with his pipe, "to cut as close to the bone as possible—"

"That's the biggest fish I've ever seen," I said. "Who caught it?"

"Your brother," said Mom. I looked up at Fred. He strained not to smile, his pipe clenched between his teeth. I smiled for both of us.

Mom pointed her knife at me. "What are you doing out of bed? I was just telling Rita about you and Frankie, and she's gonna have a word with him, you betcha!"

I looked up at Rita, and she winked at me.

"Let's scale her," said Sarge, "You'd better stand back, because these scales are going to fly."

"It's so fat," said Mom. "Is she pregnant?" This recalled something I had heard in a dream and gave me a chilly sensation of déjà vu.

"No," said Sarge. "Not this time of year. Just fat."

We stood back. Sarge went at the fish's carcass with the serrated edge of his knife, scraping off a rainbow of scales that jumped around like sequins and made everyone laugh. Dad, looking up from his paper, got my attention and nodded toward Izzy. I caught his meaning. I went to the other side of the table, where Izzy was pretending not to notice me and said, "Izzy, I'm really sorry for what I did." But I could tell the old guy's anger would not be easily soothed.

Izzy thought for a moment, while I employed my best downcast sheep-eyes. "Sorry? OK? For *vat* are you sorry, Rich'd? Say eet."

"For lying to you," I said.

"Lyink, yes. Unt vere dit you learn to lie so vell?" he asked.

"Frankie mighta taught 'im," said Rita.

Izzy turned to Rita and smiled his toothless smile.

I said, "Really, Izzy, I'm sorry for causing trouble."

"Are you done lyink?" asked Izzy. "Have you learnt you lesson?"

"I think so," I said.

Looking up, I realized Izzy and I had become the focus of attention—everyone had turned to listen to our conversation. We had upstaged Fred's fateful fish. Izzy said something to Dad in Yiddish. Dad nodded. Mom, hands on her hips, looked skeptical. Then Roland mercifully took the spotlight off me and lightened the mood in the room by limping around on his bum leg and telling the story of Fred's fight with the fish—the best fish story of the season.

WHITEY and his family moved to Northfield, on the mainland, soon after he got out of the hospital, and we did not see him for the rest of the summer. I missed him. He was all right.

I hung out with Harry, which was not so bad. We struck a bargain with Mom that if Harry were present, I was allowed to horse around on the beach and swim with Frankie and Ned. So the summer was salvaged.

Ned and Harry, an unlikely duo, became good friends. Harry had helped Ned snap out of his pitching slump on the day when Frankie and I got caught stealing and Izzy learned about Whitey and Ellen. That day, when Frankie and I left to walk the boards, Harry continued watching Ned practice. He began to announce Ned's pitches as though Ned were Jim Bunning pitching to the Pittsburgh Pirates—doing that thing he did some nights in bed by himself. Ned hurled a pitch at the painted strike zone on the wall, and Harry announced the results—as though the game were on the radio. If Ned threw a pitch with no stuff on it right down the middle to Bill Mazerosski—a piece of cake for Mazerosski—Harry announced that Maz hit a triple. When the sides changed, Ned became Vern Law.

Harry and Ned played this game almost every night for the rest of the summer, and Ned swore it restored his concentration. No doubt, Ned and Harry, transported by their nightly fantasy, could actually hear the crowd cheering and smell new-mown grass, even if the tourists walking by just saw a big kid heaving a sponge ball at a wall while another slightly chubby, delusional kid with glasses paced back and forth, waving his arms around, and calling an imaginary game as though he were By Saam.

Harry attended every game Ned pitched at Venice Park from then on. Frankie and I went along a few times too. Ned was sensational.

One morning toward the end of August, Harry proved his own athletic bona fides. He and I were on the boardwalk at the top of Vermont Avenue, assessing whether it would be a good beach day. Clouds were moving fast into the area, and we heard thunder in the distance and saw lightning over the ocean. It got darker by the minute and smelled like rain was coming. Then a bolt of lightning hit the light pole right next to us. I froze, but Harry took off down the street running so fast he easily passed a cocker spaniel running in the same direction at full tilt. Frankie happened to see all this from his porch, and he said that Harry's sprint down the block was the fastest of all time, and if we could only reproduce lightning, Harry could win at the Olympics.

THE STORM that ensued was the edge of a hurricane that hit further south. A hurricane always punctuated the end of summer. Sometimes we'd get a direct hit. For a whole day and half the night, the wind would sound like a stadium full of jeering fans. Canvas awnings and potted plants would blow clear down to Atlantic Avenue. The tide would overwhelm the beaches and surge down the streets, submerging the neighborhood calf-deep in salt water. Basement apartments would get a foot of water and require considerable renovation, though no amount of renovation could eliminate the musty smell left behind. Most often, thankfully, the hurricane would come ashore in the Carolinas and miss us. After the storm went on its way, it'd leave in its wake a few autumnal days so dry and clear you could count the windows in the Brigantine Hotel across the bay. Summer was over, but it mocked us with a few days of superb, luminous weather. These final days brought with them an odd feeling, like you no longer belonged where you were. Summer's end is always sad, and the aftermath of a hurricane, even if it misses, adds a kind of eeriness to the end of summer; it's a feeling of alienation so keen it breaks your heart. Time to go out on the beach and see what unusual treasures the storm has churned up, what marine life it has killed, and which piers had missing pieces.

On one of these crystalline mornings after the storm, the last whole day of vacation, while Mom was frying eggs, I told Harry about the trip Frankie and I took to the auction house that gave out free stuff. I'd forgotten what Frankie had called it. Fred was at the table, dressed in a shirt and tie, ready for work and happy it was his last day. He chuckled when I described the place.

"Free stuff? Where was it?" Harry asked.

"Across from Million Dollar Pier."

"Oh, you mean the jam joint?"

"Yeah, that's what Frankie called it, the 'jam joint.' Frankie claimed they kept all the money for the stuff they gave out, like radios and clocks, but I only saw them keep the money for the sewing machines and stereos. I told Frankie they gave the rest of the money back—"

"No, stupid. They kept all the money," said Harry.

"They couldn't have. I saw the guy give the dough back with the stuff. He said he was advertising—"

"But they didn't give back the important dough. You're such a bonehead! Frank took me there a couple of times. All the money is in plain view during the show. Then they grab it at the very end before they throw everyone out."

"I don't believe it."

"Don't be a sap," said Harry. "It's in the Atlantic City Press all the time. They're crooks."

"You mean, when Tex said he was giving stuff away for advertising, he was lying...?" Mom stopped scrubbing a pan in the sink and looked at the ceiling. "...And they're just a bunch of crooks?" I looked at Fred. He nodded. "So it's true," I said, "You *do* raise your hand and get fu—" Mom turned. "—Cheated. But Tex gave some people a Florida vaca—"

"—Time-share racket," said Harry, and he explained how neither the airfare nor the hotel in Florida was paid for. "It's all over the news," said Harry. "You should read the paper once in a while. The whole thing's a scam. You might get a free dinner in Florida—if you attend a sales pitch."

"Well, I'll be."

After breakfast, I saw two big yellow peaches in the refrigerator. I took them out and said to myself, "It's now or never." As the season drew to a close, having overcome my fear of stopping up for girls thanks to the Ellen episode, I started going over to CJ's place to see Marie. We'd sit on her steps and talk. She liked to sidle up to me really close, and when we touched it felt good. Today I was going to give her a peach and try for a kiss.

We were sitting on the steps. We'd finished our peaches, and wiped our hands on our bathing suits, and when she got close to me, just touching, I went in for a kiss. She let me kiss her. Our lips touched for a moment, and she was so soft and peachy, I wanted more and dove back in. But this time she pushed me away. Undaunted, I tried again. This time I got a longer kiss that sparked a delightful tingle deep inside. So I put one hand on her belly and the other around her shoulder and leaned in close for more. But this time I got a slap, right on my cheek—which was not completely unpleasant. Marie stood, though, and ran into the house, saying, "I'm not making out with a boy who is about to leave town. You shoulda kissed me two weeks ago."

I went back the next day, the day I was leaving, but Marie was not at home. At least her sisters, who couldn't stop giggling, told me she wasn't home. So that was that. I thought. Wait until Barb hears about this; she'll love it.

●

I'm going to skip the White House Sub Shop. I'll go home and eat a salad with a hard-boiled egg. I'd love a beer—a beer after the beach. Oh, Lord, please have mercy on Thy long-suffering child. Grant him a cold one without a headache....

I'll rework my list of poems tomorrow.

Maybe I'll take a sentimental journey to Vermont Avenue. I visit from time to time to see what the old neighborhood looks like. The Inlet deteriorated during my college years. It became unsafe, especially at night. In the '80s, ol' Fred wouldn't dare walk down Vermont Avenue after dark in his hip waders, carrying his beloved homemade rod and Centaur reel. The homeowners on the street, summer residents and year-rounders, including Mom and Dad, stopped living in their houses. They held on to the properties, hoping a casino would buy them and provide a windfall, but they either became slumlords and rented their houses to poor folks or, like Mom and Dad, just let the houses go. The once lively street turned bleak: The stores closed; the houses fell apart. One winter, while we were in Philadelphia, thieves broke into our house and stole the copper pipes. The next winter, an arsonist set fire to the place. The city demolished the property without even warning us. Most of the other houses on the block succumbed to the same fate. One year I visited the Inlet to see what the old neighborhood looked like, and I couldn't find Vermont Avenue. Except for the Absecon Lighthouse up at Dogshit Park, all the landmarks were gone. Everything was gone. The houses and stores had been razed—including the Vermont Apartments— and there were no street signs. I was lost—on my old street. I had to count the blocks from the end of Oriental Avenue to find which street was Vermont Avenue, and I had to count the cracked driveways from the corner to determine which house was ours. The whole Inlet neighborhood looked like a big cracked-up parking lot, strewn with every kind of weed indigenous to the Eastern Seaboard. In the distance rose the enormous, gaudy casinos that seemed to have consumed the rest of the town.

While I was trying to locate the places that were no longer there, I noticed, under a street lamp, the cement patch where Ellen had written "I love Whitey." It was still there.

JESSE married her high school sweetheart. I told her she was making a mistake. I pointed out how she'd miss all the fun of being young and single, and I warned her that her boyfriend would get restless. Barb gave me dirty looks when I remonstrated with Jesse, and said, "Leave her alone. She knows what she's doing." Mind you, I was never emphatic or harsh in my remonstrance. And I gave her and Herbert my blessing when they married, even though I was certain their early union would end badly. I was wrong. They stayed married, and they seem happy. They're both detectives in the suburbs. They have two kids. The kids are in college.

When Jesse's kids were little, I looked after them every afternoon. Jesse and Herb worked long hours, and since I was a teacher, I was free in the afternoon to pick up the kids from nursery school and care for them until Jesse or Herb came home. At first I was annoyed by this responsibility, because it impinged on my free afternoons. After work I was tired, and I wanted to go home. I considered my childcare assignment a burden. I'd already raised my own kid, I reasoned, why should I raise theirs? I didn't gripe, though. I was grandpa, and grandma was out of the picture, so I had to be grandpa and grandma. But I resented the responsibility.

I was wrong—as usual. Taking care of my grandchildren turned out to be a rewarding experience. I mattered to them. And that's important—to matter. If you don't matter, you become irrelevant. People can't stand not mattering. If you're married, you're OK, because you automatically matter to someone. And if you have a job, you're OK, because you matter to your colleagues and your clients. But if you have no one to matter to, you're in trouble. It's intolerable. People who don't matter to other people go out and get a dog, so they can at least matter to a dog; or they plant a garden, so they can matter to their plants. You have to matter! Otherwise, you'll get depressed and start to wonder why you're even here. Well, I mattered to my grandkids, and that made a difference. Truth of it is, I wish those kids were little again—they're too old now to care about grandpa, and I'm starting to feel like I don't matter any more.

One time, Jesse told me that she was jealous of her kids because I seemed to be more interested in them than I had been in her when she was growing up. She was joking, I think.

TIME to go. When Mom was old, in her eighties, she still liked a day at the beach, so I'd take her with me on my annual jaunt. This was hard because she lived pretty far from me. I spent five hours driving and only three hours on the beach. And Mom always brought a lot of supplies with her—including her heavy old chaise lounge from yesteryear. I must have looked like Tenzing Norgay, lugging all her stuff down to the beach. But she liked to bake in the sun for a few hours, albeit now fully clothed and covered with a towel and a hat. She'd lie quietly and, most likely, reminisce about summers gone by—friends with funny hats and curious recipes, hurricanes, running after babies in the shallows, gutting fish, knitting in front of the television until everyone was safe at home.... After a day of exposure to the sun, she looked as delicate and sere as a leaf in winter. I thought a sudden gust might blow her away. One time in August, as we were packing to go home, she said, "The end of a beach day always makes me sad."

I said, "Me too, especially at the end of summer." And we trudged off into the sunset, she as tiny as a child, and me hauling that unwieldy burden.

The Poems

The Song of the Wandering Aengus

I went out to the hazel wood,
Because a fire was in my head,
And cut and peeled a hazel wand,
And hooked a berry to a thread;
And when white moths were on the wing,
And moth-like stars were flickering out,
I dropped the berry in a stream
And caught a little silver trout.

When I had laid it on the floor
I went to blow the fire a-flame,
But something rustled on the floor,
And someone called me by my name:
It had become a glimmering girl
With apple blossom in her hair
Who called me by my name and ran
And faded through the brightening air.

Though I am old with wandering
Through hollow lands and hilly lands,
I will find out where she has gone,
And kiss her lips and take her hands;
And walk among long dappled grass,
And pluck till time and times are done,
The silver apples of the moon,
The golden apples of the sun.

WILLIAM BUTLER YEATS

La Belle Dame Sans Merci

O what can ail thee, knight-at-arms,
    Alone and palely loitering?
The sedge has withered from the lake,
    And no birds sing.

O what can ail thee, knight-at-arms,
    So haggard and so woe-begone?
The squirrel's granary is full,
    And the harvest's done.

I see a lily on thy brow,
    With anguish moist and fever-dew,
And on thy cheeks a fading rose
    Fast withereth too.

I met a lady in the meads,
    Full beautiful—a faery's child,
Her hair was long, her foot was light,
    And her eyes were wild.

I made a garland for her head,
    And bracelets too, and fragrant zone;
She looked at me as she did love,
    And made sweet moan

I set her on my pacing steed,
    And nothing else saw all day long,
For sidelong would she bend, and sing
    A faery's song.

She found me roots of relish sweet,
    And honey wild, and manna-dew,
And sure in language strange she said—
    'I love thee true'.

She took me to her Elfin grot,
    And there she wept and sighed full sore,
And there I shut her wild wild eyes
    With kisses four.

And there she lullèd me asleep,
    And there I dreamed—Ah! woe betide!—
The latest dream I ever dreamt
    On the cold hill side.

I saw pale kings and princes too,
    Pale warriors, death-pale were they all;
They cried—'La Belle Dame sans Merci
    Thee hath in thrall!'

I saw their starved lips in the gloam,
    With horrid warning gapèd wide,
And I awoke and found me here,
    On the cold hill's side.

And this is why I sojourn here,
    Alone and palely loitering,
Though the sedge is withered from the lake,
    And no birds sing.

JOHN KEATS

Sonnet LXIV
When I have seen by Time's fell hand defac'd

When I have seen by Time's fell hand defac'd
The rich-proud cost of outworn buried age;
When sometime lofty towers I see down-razed
And brass eternal, slave to mortal rage;
When I have seen the hungry ocean gain
Advantage on the kingdom of the shore,
And the firm soil win of the wat'ry main,
Increasing store with loss, and loss with store;
When I have seen such interchange of state,
Or state itself confounded to decay;
Ruin hath taught me thus to ruminate—
That Time will come and take my love away.
This thought is as a death, which cannot choose
But weep to have that which it fears to lose.

WILLIAM SHAKESPEARE

Nothing Gold Can Stay

Nature's first green is gold,
Her hardest hue to hold.
Her early leaf's a flower;
But only so an hour.
Then leaf subsides to leaf.
So Eden sank to grief,
So dawn goes down to day.
Nothing gold can stay.

ROBERT FROST

Loveliest of Trees

176

Loveliest of trees, the cherry now
Is hung with bloom along the bough,
And stands about the woodland ride
Wearing white for Eastertide.

Now, of my threescore years and ten,
Twenty will not come again,
And take from seventy springs a score,
It only leaves me fifty more.

And since to look at things in bloom
Fifty springs are little room,
About the woodlands I will go
To see the cherry hung with snow.

A.E. Housman

RICHARD ADELMAN is a resident of Philadelphia. He taught English in public high schools there for thirty-seven years. While teaching, Richard worked on weekends as a wedding photographer and, during the summer, he worked as a restaurant manager in Atlantic City. He is presently retired and developing a comic strip at **terryandblueberry.com**.

Photo: Cheryl Fedyna

Acknowledgments

I'd like to thank the following people and one entity: My friend Mike Herr gave me a lot of advice on style. Jeff Cushner helped me remember some of the details about AC in '63. My brother Harv also helped me remember things. Rubin Naiman and Jack Weisel helped with the Yiddish. My old friend and colleague Cheryl Fedyna encouraged me to write the original version of this book, an unfinished project that languished in a drawer for thirty years. Many thanks to Andy Biscontini and Wyatt Doyle for their collegiality and editorial support. Finally, I need to thank the Public School Employees' Retirement System and all those who made it possible for me to be a member of that organization, for providing me with a pension that helps me pay my bills and pursue leisure activities like novel writing in my old age.

"I am displaced"
An excerpt from Richard Adelman's
TEACHER TALES

MY LAST year, during third period, my lunch period, when I normally had my room to myself, a hitch in my roster forced me to eat lunch in the English office across the hall instead of in my own room, because a "floating" teacher, Miss Rigg, came into my room that period and displaced me. In previous years I could spread out during third period. I could eat a leisurely lunch, read a magazine, do some paperwork, straighten the room—do whatever was necessary. I had the whole room to myself; no one bothered me. I could close the door and be invisible. I can't tell you how my heart sank the first day of the year when Miss Rigg and a group of her students, eleventh graders, invaded my room when I was about to eat lunch and relax.

"I'm your new roomie," piped young Miss Rigg, steering a cart full of papers and books into the room. Her flimsy dress and unrestrained hair showed how lately the summer had ended. She beamed and pointed toward the front of the room. "Can I use this section of the chalkboard?"

"I suppose so," I said, and I felt the first stirrings of anxiety.

A floating teacher is a teacher without a room of her own, who must encamp throughout the day in other teachers' rooms. She wheels her cart full of supplies—her portable classroom—into the room of a teacher who has the period free, followed by a swarm of noisy teenagers, and the regular occupant (in this case me) needs to find a place to bivouac. So, from that first day on, when the floating teacher entered my room, I hastily gathered my things—my banana, my apple, my snack bar, my computer, and some papers to grade—and I retreated to the English office—with every intention of doing what I would normally do in my own room. And that's how I got to know Mr. Wood and Mrs. Worthington. We met every third period in the small English department office and had lunch together. At first I kept to myself while I ate my meager lunch, but after a while I found myself in idle conversation with my new friends.

The English office was as crowded as an antique shop. It was primarily the office of Mrs. Hegel, the department chair. She organized the department's business on the top of her desk using piles of papers, stacked one atop another, crosswise, to distinguish one pile from the next. These piles grew higher and higher—I have no idea what they contained—and there were quite a few of them, so that the actual work area on her desk was a small one-foot square, just enough space to set down a paper and scribble a signature. These paper piles of Hegel's accumulated as the year went by and, once they reached the tipping point on her desk, they migrated to the window sill, the top of her file cabinet, her computer table, and a rolling cart that she brought into the office to accommodate the overflow. Finally these towering stacks began to reproduce on the teachers' worktable, which might otherwise seat three or four teachers comfortably were it not for the towers. My lunchmates and I sat at this table, and at times I could only see them from the chin up. The office also housed the department's photocopy machine, which produced its own stacks of papers—the mistakes and extras that hurried teachers discarded, along with the reams and reams of blank sheets waiting to be used. Also, the office was the hub for sets of books that teachers returned after borrowing them to distribute to their students. Piles of *The Iliad* teetered next to piles of *The Catcher in the Rye* and collapsed into towers of *Brave New World*. These stacks of books were piled on file cabinets that held the department's archives of tests on all these works of literature (which I never used, since the answer sheets were always missing). Finally, the room was surrounded on three sides by dusty bookshelves that held all manner of educational relics: reference books, old VHS tapes, sample copies of texts from vendors, and some antique tomes that a rare book dealer might find interesting. I once brought down a copy of *The Innocents Abroad* that had only one copyright date. Since I was alone in the office when I found this antique, I slipped it into my briefcase and added it to my personal library at home, knowing no one would notice it missing.

I think you can see how crowded the room was, but Chairwoman Hegel's husband applied the finishing touch to the décor by moving his desk into the cramped office. Although he was a social studies teacher, his affection and allegiance to his wife compelled him to take up residence next to her with a facing desk, and he used the same filing system as she—stacks of crisscrossed papers. Additionally, he was a devotee of the hands-on approach to teaching history; that is, he assigned his students the making of historical models and dioramas. His corner of the office was crowded with reproductions of famous icons that his students generated—the Wright Brothers' Flyer, the Roman Coliseum, knights in shining armor, Viking ships—and these, like all the papers and books, multiplied around the room as the year progressed, some of them produced by desperate students more adept at crafts than scholarship, who hoped to improve their grades by increasing the size of their models, until their efforts were almost life-sized. Yes, a life-sized sarcophagus of King Tut would not have surprised us if we saw it propped in the corner of the room behind Mr. Hegel's desk.

It was close quarters in that office, and dust lay everywhere. On the odd occasion when Mr. Hegel drew the ancient curtains that hung beside the windows, motes of dust as thick as schools of minnows swam through the shafts of light.

Luckily, during the period when my colleagues and I ate lunch, Mr. and Mrs. Hegel had classes to teach, so we were able to sit at the worktable and chat unsupervised. The Hegels were always eager to socialize with whomever they hosted in their office and, pulling rank, they were apt to hold court from the superior position of their desks and dominate the discussion. But the cat was away during this period, so we mice could do as we pleased.

Mr. Wood was somewhere past the middle of his career, in his forties, I guessed. A bit shabby, he wore jeans with a sport jacket and a buttoned-down shirt. He was getting to the age when a person needs to come to terms with the reality that his metabolism cannot cope with all the calories he consumes. His clothes were getting tight around the middle. Destined for baldness, he let his blond hair grow long, though not like a vagabond, more like a man who told his barber he was opting for long hair, and he combed it straight back. In his face I could see he had once been handsome; he had a definable jaw and a sparkle in his eye.

At the beginning, when Wood and I sat across the table from one another and said little, I knew him only by the surprising lunches he brought. These lunches denied his lapsed youth. He was partial to processed meats, combined with cheese, on white bread. He liked a hoagie from the Wawa or a cheesesteak from the truck down the street; there was ham (with a variety of spicy edges) combined with fragrant cheeses, and there was bologna and American with mayo, even liverwurst and onion. I was a little jealous, I must admit, because I remembered the time, long ago, when I would enjoy such lunches, before my doctors outlawed them and Mrs. Kessler stopped preparing them. For the last twenty years of my career, my lunch consisted of the same three items: a banana, an apple, and a snack bar (thank God for the luxury of the snack bar or I think I'd have gone insane). But Wood ate without restrictions. His chips were the high octane variety—deep fried in trans fat, not baked.

One day early in the year, as I was scoring tests, Mr. Wood unwrapped his lunch, and I was unsure what kind of sandwich he had, though I scrutinized it carefully, as usual. It had a familiar aroma.

"What's for lunch, Mr. Wood?" I asked.

Studying the edge of the sandwich, Wood replied, "Lebanon bologna and some kind of cheese." He dug in.

This sent me reeling. As I bit into my banana, I recalled the pleasures I had taken years ago with this same salty delicacy, so fatty and piquant. "I used to combine Lebanon bologna with cream cheese," I said, "And I would vary the types of cream cheese. I remember it was particularly good with chive cream cheese," and when I said this I felt the kind of tingle a boy feels when he sees a girl in clothes he likes. I resolved to stop at the supermarket on the way home and get a quarter pound of Lebanon bologna and a tub of cream cheese and eat it that very night. But I didn't.

"Hmm, sounds good," said Wood. "I might just try that."

Every day Mr. Wood unwrapped his lunch and filled the cluttered office with the aromas of garlicky cold cuts, with onions sprinkled with oregano and soaked in oil, and various cheeses—cheddar, Havarti, provolone—while I brooded on a diet of fruit and paperwork.

Usually, young Mrs. Worthington joined us for lunch. She ate a big salad, swimming in creamy dressings of every color, from a Tupperware container. But she often didn't stay for the whole period, unless Mr. Wood had launched into one of his stories, which were irresistible. Worthington was younger than we and had important work to do in the school. Although she was a teacher, she had acquired administrative duties, owing no doubt to her youth, her charm, her exuberance for her job, and her recent schooling in all the modern methods of education. She was lithe and energetic, dressed in tailored pinstriped suits— seemingly never the same suit twice, nor the same silk shirt, nor the same necklace (how did she do that?). She wore her hair in a short, natural Afro, which suited the efficiency she needed for her ambitious pursuits. She was on all kinds of committees and action groups—a real go-getter, and a reliable resource for Mr. Wood, who never read a memo and would never have known what was due or what was going on in the school without her. When she sat, she introduced a welcome whiff of lilies to the room—until she pried open her Tupperware.

Thinking back, my greatest regret was what happened between Mrs. Worthington and me, although I made a mess of my friendship with Mr. Wood, too.

Our first real conversation—other than about food or memos— resulted from Wood's saying something that I found particularly annoying. He launched into a lengthy explanation about how he planned to approach the next novel he planned to teach. My belief always was that teachers should not share ideas. Everyone knows what works for him, I thought, so it is counterproductive to hear the ideas of others. I always hated when a colleague wanted to discuss his teaching methods. I cringed when a fellow teacher at a teachers' meeting would raise his hand and start in with the words *"What I do is...."* I always wished such palaverers would just shut up. Not only did no one care what the know-it-all had to say, but the objective of a teachers' meeting has always been to get it finished as swiftly as possible, and I did not appreciate any unnecessary nattering, like questions and suggestions. I often closed my eyes during meetings and, if I were lucky, drifted off to sleep.

To my mind, Mr. Wood was breaking one of the cardinal rules of teacher interaction by talking about curriculum at lunch, and this gave me a negative early impression of him. He looked up from his Jewish salami sandwich, which may or may not have been on a twisted roll, and he asked, "Do you teach *The Color Purple*?"

"Yes," I said, "I teach it every year."

"You know," he said, swallowing and licking a bit of mustard from his thumb, "I think Alice Walker made this book too easy. The moral reasoning in *The Color Purple* is too clear. There's good and there's bad. But nothing in life is that clear. I've been thinking that I will present the idea that *The Color Purple* is an example of a novel that deconstructs commonly held beliefs. I think I can show how the book deconstructs myths—myths about women, and blacks, and even ugly people. Then we can work with the idea of deconstruction rather than the text. Deconstruction itself will be the focus. I can't deal with a book that depicts such moral clarity."

"What's the matter with clarity?" I asked, though I should have said nothing. Saying nothing is the best way to thwart a conversation. But I joined in, "I have taught *The Color Purple* for years," I said. "The kids like it. It's a book about an underdog who winds up on top. What's wrong with that? Guy beats up girl; guy gets his comeuppance. It's a book about a bully. The bully should always get it in the end. Pretty clear, no?"

"There is some moral ambiguity in the character of Shug. She's a righteous sinner," said Worthington, packing her briefcase and preparing to leave, "but if I taught *The Color Purple* I'd concentrate on the social issues. I think the social issues in the book *are* morally unambiguous but worth getting into."

Mercifully, Wood resumed ruminating on his idea of deconstruction (whatever that is) silently. His salami sandwich, I noted, looked like it contained slices that he actually cut from a miniature salami. "Sometimes the best parts of the book are in the subtexts," he mused. And I thought, *Poor kids. I'm glad I'm not in that class. What the hell are subtexts?* But I said, "You should go with that deconstruction thing. I think it will go well."

Teacher Tales is available in softcover and deluxe hardcover editions.

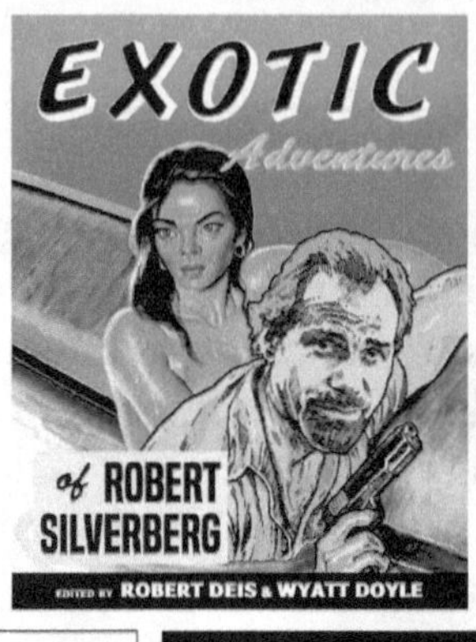

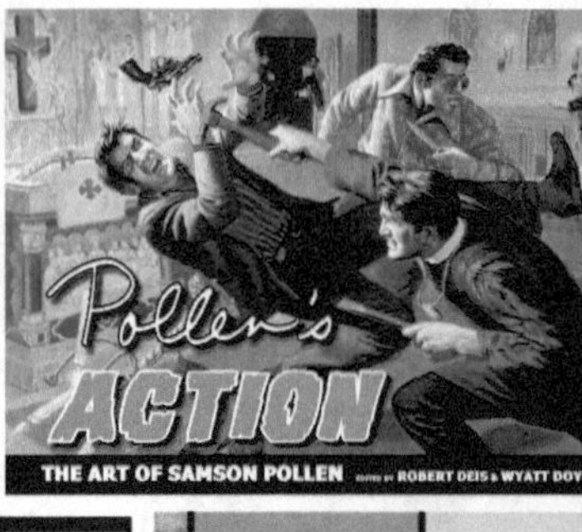

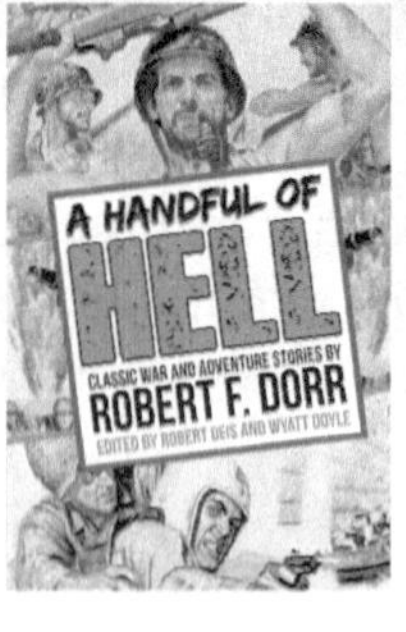

Words and Pictures and Music

Words and Pictures and Music

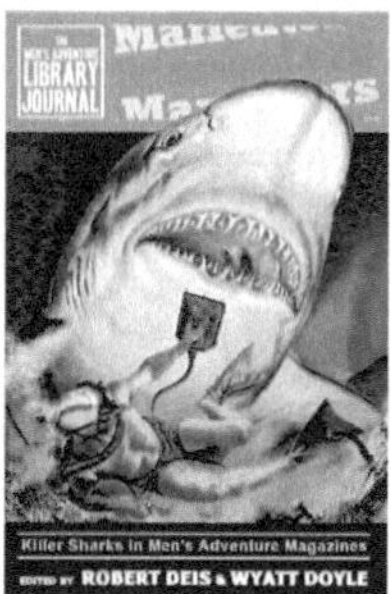

new texture

new texture